ACTS

A Screenplay

with The Book of Life and Soon

ACTS

A Screenplay

with The Book of Life and Soon

Hal Hartley

with a foreword by
Dr. Jacqueline Bussie

ELBORO

For over a decade I have taught Hal Hartley's 1998 film *The Book of Life* both in the Theology curriculum and in my Religion and Film courses. No other film out there can rival its brilliant exploration of the (largely unpopular) theological concept of universalism. In that brisk-paced short feature, Jesus returns to earth but refuses to enact the anticipated apocalyptic judgment, opting instead for radical, universal forgiveness—much to the chagrin of God's lawyers and many devout Christians who cherish their identity as 'the saved.'

Acts exhibits many of the same refreshing and insightful qualities that characterize *The Book of Life*—thematic threads of theological universalism, Hartley's fiercely independent and liberating hermeneutic, a painfully honest portrayal of human complexity, and a noteworthy examination of Christianity's ambivalence in history. Every page of *Acts* is permeated with the classic *Hartleyesque* irreverent reverence for all things metaphysical, for all issues of 'ultimate concern,' to borrow a term from theologian Paul Tillich.

From my perspective as a Christian theologian, Christianity has lost much of its original playfulness and humility without which many of its followers fall into dangerous positions of self-righteousness and religious imperialism. Hartley's irreverent reverence in *Acts* provides a very helpful countertext to these forms of theological arrogance. The screenplay's ambiguous protagonist, the apostle Paul, both repulses and fascinates the reader. Like many Hartley protagonists, Paul in *Acts* is both hero and antihero. Yet this portrayal is theological to its core, in that it calls to mind Martin Luther's famous depiction of human beings as '*simul justus et peccator*'—simultaneously saint and sinner. On the one hand, Paul is cocky, fanatical, and masochistic, but on the other, he is self-effacing, radically inclusive, and admirably dedicated to his faith.

Willing to die as a martyr for his beliefs, this Paul—unlike the stereotypical fundamentalist—is nevertheless eminently teachable, and throughout the screenplay reveals himself as capable of change and self-reckoning. In short, Paul is *simul* religious fanatic and teachable truth seeker. As walking oxymoron, his character embodies the best and the worst of Christianity. Indeed, throughout the screenplay, Hartley himself critiques Christianity and its institutionalized distortions, but somehow simultaneously distills Christianity down to a salvageable and beautiful, albeit controversial, essence: "These Jesus Followers," a character complains, "preach nothing but the forgiveness of sins—a recipe for absolute anarchy!"

Many scholars argue that Jesus' parables, in their original context, must have made his audiences laugh out loud. In this imaginative resituating of the New Testament book, *The Acts of the Apostles*, Hartley manages to suggest the recognizably human motivations—petty, misguided, often hilarious—behind what has become biblical legend. It can make you laugh out loud and engage in meaningful theological reflection at the same time—a rare and compelling combination.

Dr. Jacqueline Bussie

Executive Director
Collegeville Institute for Ecumenical and Cultural Research
Collegeville, Minnesota

ACTS

001. EXTERIOR, ROME STREETS—DAY

A young man, Luke, crosses a busy street, dodges automobile traffic and enters a building. Although the surroundings are perfectly modern, a title card announces: *Rome, 64 Common Era.*

002. INTERIOR, NEWSPAPER OFFICE—DAY

Luke comes through the rows of desks, nodding hello to friends, then stops and knocks on an office's doorframe. Theo looks up from the newspaper he's reading and waves him in.

> LUKE
>
> What's up?

> THEO
>
> Luke! Come in. Same old same old. Scandals, coups, assassinations, a little human interest here and there. But the big news is, of course, the fire.

> LUKE
>
> They say three districts of the city are in ruins.

> THEO
>
> It's been suggested that the emperor did it himself to clear space for new building projects.

> LUKE
>
> That's highly unlikely.

> THEO
>
> Of course, but that's not our concern. As we know from past experience, someone needs to be blamed so as to discredit this accusation. Heads must roll.

> LUKE
>
> Who do you think it will be?

                    THEO
Correct question! That's why you're here. It
will be the city's Jews, I'm certain. But, as a
certain fly on the wall up on the hill tells me
it'll be this unknown, weird little sect of
Judaism called…
          (consults notes)
Christians.

                    LUKE
Ah. I see.

Theo stands and comes around his desk, he lights a cigarette and
sits beside Luke on the couch.

                    THEO
What do you know? What can you tell me
about these people—these Christians?

                    LUKE
I met Paul, oh, it must be five years ago now.

                    THEO
And who's he?

                    LUKE
The Apostle to the Gentiles.

                    THEO
A Jew?

                    LUKE
Yes. He was important to this whole Jesus
movement.

                    THEO
And who's that?

                    LUKE
Jesus? Oh, it's a long story. And it's all
tied up with this guy Paul.

THEO
(stands)
Well then, get to work. I need fifteen
hundred to two thousand words for the
Friday edition. Who are these Jews who
call themselves Christians, who is this
guy Paul? What's his relationship with
this—what's his name?

LUKE

Jesus.

THEO

Jesus. And what's the likelihood that they
had something to do with the fire here in
Rome last week.
(snaps his fingers)
Go!

003. INTERIOR, BAR—DAY

Phoebe, the bartender, is sorting through a shoebox full of corres-
pondence. She gets Luke another beer and places one particular
letter out on the bar before him.

PHOEBE

This is the letter he wrote to us from Ephesus.
I carried it here to Rome myself. We pass them
around, each group to another.

LUKE
(studies letter)
There are others?

PHOEBE

Groups? Oh, we're all over.
(finds a second letter)
Here, this is to the church at Corinth.
(finds more)
This one is to the Philippians. Ephesians.
Oh, Galatians! Look. That's a good one.

LUKE

It's okay I read them?

PHOEBE

Sure. You say you met him?

LUKE

Yeah, on Malta in fifty-nine. He was on his
way here to Rome to stand trial.

PHOEBE

What was he like?

LUKE

You didn't know him?

PHOEBE

I met him in Ephesus, briefly, seven or eight
years ago, when he gave me that letter. We
waited for him here, but he never showed up.

Luke takes the box of letters and his beer over to a table and starts reading.

004. EXTERIOR, JERUSALEM PARKING LOT—DAY

A rugged, intense and recklessly emotional 35-year-old man, Paul, cuffs the hands of a defiant younger guy named Stephen. Paul then steps back and gestures for his comrades to take Stephen away. They do. A title card announces: *Jerusalem, 32 Common Era.* Paul steps aside and lights a cigarette, troubled. Behind him we see his truck with the company's name emblazoned across it: *Paul of Tarsus, Tentmaker.*

005. INTERIOR, JERUSALEM TEMPLE—DAY

Paul and his gang drag Stephen into the assembly hall followed by a rabble of curiosity seekers and journalists. Paul falls into a seat and follows the proceedings inattentively. Up at the front of the hall are three Jewish priests who are judges. Stephen stands before them. A representative of the outraged citizenry points to the prisoner.

ACCUSER
This man, Stephen, never stops saying
things against the Temple and the Law. He is
a follower of the blasphemer, Jesus. He speaks
in his name and says this Jesus will rise from
the dead and destroy the Temple and change
the customs handed down to us from Moses.

GIDEON
(a priest, sorts through papers)
Jesus… from Nazareth. I've got it here somewhere. Hold on…

JOSEPHUS
(also a priest, clarifies)
A political agitator. He made things difficult
for us with the Romans.

PARMENAS
(the third priest, by rote)
Stephen, we understand there is a small
community of people who have dedicated
themselves to the memory of this Jesus
person. Since the time of Julius Caesar, however, our Roman overlords have granted us
Jews certain freedoms in regard to our
customs and beliefs. We, the high priests of
the Temple, must safeguard those freedoms
by punishing Jews who press too violently
against the status quo.

STEPHEN
We are forever opposing the Holy Spirit—
just as our ancestors did.

PARMENAS
(easygoing)
We are a stiff-necked people, it is true. But
we abide by the prophets.

STEPHEN
But which of the prophets have we not
persecuted?

PARMENAS
Enough.

STEPHEN
Even Moses!

GIDEON
(warns)
Easy, son.

STEPHEN
(recites)
"God will raise up a prophet for you from
amongst your own people, just as he has
raised me up!"

PARMENAS
Stephen, if I had a coin for every troublemaker
who comes through here claiming to be the
prophet Moses predicted I'd be a very, very
rich man.

STEPHEN
Even Moses! We pushed him aside and made
idols of gold and silver to worship!

GIDEON
A regrettable episode but far in the past.

STEPHEN
We kill those who foretell the coming of the
Righteous One!

JOSEPHUS
(intrigued)
And so you insist that this Jesus of Nazareth
was the Righteous One.

STEPHEN
He is the Messiah come to redeem Israel.

The people murmur angrily.

PARMENAS
Let us grant, for the sake of argument, that
this is true: Jesus was the Messiah.

STEPHEN
He *is* the Messiah.

JOSEPHUS
Stephen, the man is dead.

STEPHEN
He rose from the dead and ascended into
heaven.

The place shakes with argument and outrage. Paul sits forward, elbows on his knees, and tugs at his hair.

ACCUSER
You see! You see what I mean!

PARMENAS
Now, *that* is, in fact, blasphemous.

GIDEON
Stephen, belief in resurrection is blasphemy.
Say you didn't mean it.

STEPHEN
But I did mean it.

PARMENAS
Stephen.

PAUL
You Sadducees believe it is blasphemy. We
Pharisees do not.

                         GIDEON
          Yeah, well who's in charge here, you Pharisees
          or us? Sit the fuck down!

Paul walks outside to have a smoke, disgusted. But he pauses in
the doorway and listens as—

                         JOSEPHUS
                      (to Stephen)
          Why would God have chosen this man, Jesus,
          as the Messiah, the deliverer of Israel, if he
          was not even able to save himself from such
          abject defeat? He was nailed to a cross by the
          Romans, for cryin' out loud. A disgrace!

Paul waits with the others for Stephen's reply. But the young man
doesn't answer.

                        PARMENAS
                      (gives up)
          Take him away!

                         GIDEON
                   (reads the sentence)
          You are a blasphemer! Condemned to death
          by stoning.

Paul shakes his head, lights his cigarette and walks out.

006. EXTERIOR, JERUSALEM—DAY

Temple functionaries tie Stephen to a large concrete slab at the
foot of a three-story-tall building, still under construction. Up on
the building, others are busy positioning a crane that dangles
another large two-ton concrete slab over the victim. Up top, by the
crane, Paul sits watching. Once Stephen is tied fast, the functionaries stand aside and the young man calls out—

                         STEPHEN
                       (scared)
          Lord, do not hold this sin against them!

But the sign is given and those up on the building release the crane's brake. Stephen screams and Paul turns away as he hears the falling slab splatter the young man. He notices the priest, Josephus, standing away to the side, looking down at the carnage.

JOSEPHUS

(shrugs)
The Law.

PAUL

Who was he?

JOSEPHUS

(turns away)
These Jesus Followers make things bad for everyone.

PAUL

I hear they preach nothing but the forgiveness of sins.

JOSEPHUS

A recipe for absolute anarchy.

PAUL

They don't seem like violent people.

JOSEPHUS

Neither did their prophet.

PAUL

You remember him?

JOSEPHUS

I remember his arraignment.

PAUL

His reputation is strong out there in the suburbs.

JOSEPHUS

He was a great healer, they say.

PAUL
Did he himself actually say he was the Messiah?

JOSEPHUS
Not that I can remember. He was not a blasphemer.
He was executed by the Romans for sedition.

They reach the other end of the building and look out over the killing fields: hundreds of people hanging from crosses.

PAUL
How is it possible a young man like that
becomes a threat to the empire?

JOSEPHUS
(not interested)
We hear you're continuing on towards
Damascus.

PAUL
I've made tents I have to deliver to the Roman
Army just east of the city.

JOSEPHUS
There is a group of Jesus Followers stirring
up trouble in Damascus.
(holds out an envelope)
Here's a communiqué from the high priest to
the synagogue there explaining your mission
to track them down—men and women—and
bring them, bound, to Jerusalem.

PAUL
Why me?

JOSEPHUS
Why *not* you? You're usually the first one to
volunteer.

PAUL
I ain't got the stomach for it anymore.

JOSEPHUS
They are blasphemers.

PAUL
(tosses away cigarette)
And what the hell does that mean! There
are seven or eight different versions of the
Hebrew religion in this one city alone and
none of us can agree on anything!

JOSEPHUS
Argument is required. Debate. The scriptures
need to be interpreted. What's wrong with that?

PAUL
Look, I am the most devout Jew that ever lived.
Anywhere. And if I've been doing the Temple's
dirty work and chasing down these Jesus
Followers, it's only because I know we have to
perfect ourselves before the Messiah will arrive.

JOSEPHUS
Perfection won't come in a flash, Paul.

This kind of talk irritates Paul. He looks at his hands.

PAUL
No, but God's judgment will. Whether the
Messiah comes or not.

JOSEPHUS
Is it any wonder we ask you to maintain order?
Paul, true, few are as zealous as you, or as civic
minded. But fewer still are as tough.
(insists as Paul turns away)
We are God's chosen people because we have
the law. And the law must be protected. That's
the only way towards perfection.
(approaches as Paul thinks)
This is the list. Just this one last time. Please.
No one else is available.

PAUL
(takes envelope)
I leave in the morning.

007. EXTERIOR, JERUSALEM STREETS—DAY

Paul walks back to his hotel through the streets. He notices a prostitute trailing along beside him.

PROSTITUTE
Hey handsome, wanna date?

PAUL
Leave me alone!

PROSTITUTE
Fuck off, asshole!

He turns a corner and suddenly stops short. Before him is a malnourished mother clutching her diseased and disfigured child.

MOTHER
Please, sir, please, can you give us something?
Something, please…

Unnerved, Paul drops some coins in the woman's lap and hurries on. But he's almost knocked down when the back door of a bar is thrown open and two men dive out into the street, deep into a vicious fistfight. A bunch of kids on the roof above cheer the two fighters on. Paul waits for an opportunity to rush past. Once he has, he comes around the corner into another alley where a couple of junkies desperately prepare to shoot up as, ten feet away, two drunks wrestle over a bottle of booze and fall in the mud. Shaking his head clear and gasping for air, Paul makes it to the far end of the alley only to find the kids from the rooftop have now jumped down and are throwing firecrackers at a dog tied to a lamppost. He chases the little bastards away and unties the dog which, in its terror, lunges for him and bites his hand. As the animal runs off Paul inspects the wound. He sees a drainpipe spilling rainwater from off the roof into a barrel. He goes over and holds his hand under the flowing water. Calming down, he glances in through the greasy broken window of an apartment and sees four or five people fornicating wildly: men and women, men and men, women and women. He turns aside in disgust and goes on his way.

008. INTERIOR, JERUSALEM DELI—DAY

Paul stops in to buy more cigarettes. The cashier behind the counter is gossiping with a customer—

> CASHIER
> She's a slut and he has no idea. I saw her
> with the neighbor's kid the other day.

> CUSTOMER
> No!

> CASHIER
> Yes. She poses nude for his friend the
> photographer.

Paul pays and leaves with his smokes. In the doorway, though, he steps aside and makes way for a young man just finishing saying to his friend—

> YOUNG MAN
> *(outraged)*
> I'm gonna kill him!

> FRIEND
> Calm down.

> YOUNG MAN
> Did you see what he wrote in the paper?

> FRIEND
> He's allowed to have an opinion.

> YOUNG MAN
> He should be put up against the wall and shot!

Practically suffocating, Paul continues on his way.

009. INTERIOR, JERUSALEM SYNAGOGUE—DAY

Troubled, Paul confides to the local rabbi—

PAUL
There's blood on my hands.

GAMALIEL
Your deeds are righteous before the Lord.

PAUL
Did you ever meet this guy Jesus?

GAMALIEL
I heard him talk once or twice. A nice guy.
A little too otherworldly for me, though. I
suggested he steer clear of politics but in the
end, of course, you know he was disgraced.

PAUL
His brother James has a group here in Jerusalem
somewhere.

GAMALIEL
They're considered heretics, but they're
tolerated for the time being. Do you need
information?

PAUL
(stands and leaves)
No.

010. INTERIOR, JERUSALEM HOTEL ROOM—NIGHT

Paul enters the room and falls down on the bed, covering his eyes
with his hand. Finally, he rolls onto his side and stares at the wall.
The streetlight coming through the windowpanes has cast the
shadow of a cross on this wall. He contemplates this then gets up
and sits at the little desk, reaching for a pen and opening his notebook. He stares at the blank page for a moment. He hesitates, but
then lifts his pen. All at once, in two swift strokes, he draws a

vertical line and a horizontal—a cross.

011. EXTERIOR, DAMASCUS HIGHWAY—DAY

Paul and his employees are traveling along the road to Damascus. It's a major convoy comprising three big tractor trailers. The lead truck turns off into a rest stop. The others follow.

012. EXTERIOR, DAMASCUS TRUCK STOP—DAY

Paul climbs down from the lead truck, staring at the ground as though he has forgotten something. His second-in-command, Gus, climbs down from the next truck and passes by before noticing that Paul looks deeply troubled. The other drivers, though, turn back and watch as Paul looks up at the sky and then around himself at the highway, the parking lot and the urban blight in the distance. Gus, too, now stops and looks on. They can see he is becoming increasingly agitated and, though he looks across at them, he can't speak. He starts trembling, sweating, and becomes unsteady on his feet. The drivers come closer, concerned, but stop when Paul falls to the ground and has an epileptic fit. The drivers look at Gus.

                    GUS
          This happens sometimes.

Gus breaks a fallen branch over his knee and forces a piece of it between Paul's teeth. He steps back and, with the others, watches as Paul's fit runs its course. One of the drivers moves closer to assist the fallen man but Gus stops him and gestures that it is not safe. Everyone falls back a step. Paul lies there on the ground, shaking, murmuring inarticulately, and staring out across the pavement at something only he can see.

013. EXTERIOR, DAMASCUS MARKET—DAY

A twenty-year-old man named Adam is seated in the shade of the marketplace. He overhears two saleswomen discussing Paul.

                    RACHEL
          Who is he?

                    SARAH
They say he was sent by the high priest in
Jerusalem to find followers of Jesus and to
bring them to Jerusalem.

                    RACHEL
Was he always blind?

                    SARAH
No, they say it happened on the road. He fell
down, trembling, and couldn't talk anymore
either.

                    RACHEL
He's possessed by a devil.

                    SARAH
He hasn't eaten in three days. I'm afraid he'll
die right there in the house.

Adam approaches and lifts a piece of fruit from Sarah's cart.

                    SARAH
Hello Adam.

                    ADAM
              (hands her a coin)
Hello Sarah. Is everything all right?

                    SARAH
My father let some men from Jerusalem stay
at our house. One of them is sick.

                    ADAM
The headman?

                    SARAH
Yes. Paul's his name, I think.

Rachel steps aside and glances up the street. Returning, she busies
herself with her wares, speaking softly—

RACHEL
Be careful Adam. They're looking for
people like you.

This surprises Sarah. She looks from her friend to the young man.

014. EXTERIOR, DAMASCUS STREET—DAY

Adam flits through the crowd inconspicuously and finds a seclud-
ed doorway where he can sit down and think a moment.

015. INTERIOR, DAMASCUS HOME—DAY

Adam appears in the doorway. An old woman approaches.

GRANDMOTHER
Yes?

ADAM
I am here to see the man named Paul.

The grandmother looks aside to Gus. He comes forward.

GUS
Who are you?

ADAM
A friend.

GUS
He's sick.

ADAM
Perhaps I can help him.

Gus glances up and down the street before allowing Adam to
enter. He leads him through the large home to a back room.

016. INTERIOR, DAMASCUS HOME—DAY

Paul is lying on a cot, still sweating and trembling, staring with unseeing eyes at the wall a few inches from his face. Adam comes closer. Another one of Paul's companions, Simon, looks to Gus.

                         SIMON
            Who's this?

                          GUS
            An exorcist.

                         ADAM
                     (protests)
            No!

They look at him suspiciously. He braces himself, glances back once more at Paul, and then announces—

                         ADAM
            He is filled with the spirit of Jesus.

Gus and Simon are disgusted.

                          GUS
            Holy shit. I can't believe this!

                         ADAM
            It is Jesus who has spoken to him!

Gus steps forward, backhands Adam across the face, and the kid falls to the floor without a sound. But it is Paul who convulses as if hit. Adam shakes his head clear and tries to get up.

                          GUS
            Tie the fool up and put him outside.

Simon grabs a rope, kicks Adam in the ribs, and is about to tie his hands behind his back when Paul sits up from the cot. Gus is dumbfounded. Simon is scared. Adam has to look back over his shoulder to see what the sudden silence is all about.

                          GUS
            Paul?

PAUL

Why do you persecute me?

GUS

Paul, it's us.

PAUL
(dazed)
I am Jesus whom you are persecuting.

Simon and Gus look at one another, then over at Adam. Paul sits up at the edge of the cot, staring blindly before himself at nothing until Adam slowly gets up off the floor and comes over. Hesitating, he reaches out his hands and places them over Paul's eyes. At his touch, Paul falls forward into Adam's arms, startling the young man. Confused and uncertain, Adam holds Paul as he sobs.

017. EXTERIOR, DAMASCUS HOME—DAY

A few days later, Paul is recovering. He sits in the backyard with Adam who helps him drink. Paul sips the water and leans back, watching Adam.

ADAM

I don't know why I did it.

PAUL

But you knew who I was—why I had come here.

ADAM

I was afraid. It's true. But I was just all of a sudden perfectly confident you would listen to me.

PAUL

You're brave.

ADAM
(modestly)
I have learned to follow the prompting of my heart.

PAUL

Of course you're crazy too. But you are brave.
(looks across at his employees)
Look at them: they're scared of you now.

Adam looks over at Simon and Gus and sees them cower back, wary. He looks back at Paul and follows the older man's gaze to a group of neighbors standing by the fence, watching them from the next yard.

PAUL

Imagine what they're thinking: The one who
has been persecuting us is now proclaiming
the faith.

Adam leans forward and grips Paul's wrist.

ADAM

You are an instrument whom the Lord has chosen.

Paul keeps his eyes on the neighbors. Then, looking at his new friend, admits—

PAUL

I know.

018. EXTERIOR, DAMASCUS STREET—DAY

Crowds gather and follow as Paul makes his way to the local synagogue.

019. INTERIOR, DAMASCUS SYNAGOGUE—DAY

Small groups of people throughout the room stop and look on as Paul enters with the crowd behind him.

PAUL

(loudly)
God has decreed that the end of days is near.

No one is impressed. And Paul is a clumsy public speaker. He clears his throat and tries again.

                    PAUL
              (continues)
Israel is to be redeemed. The long procession
of prophets and holy men in the scriptures
have always pointed to a coming anointed one:
a messiah. The Messiah has come. He was
called Jesus and he came from Nazareth.

Some men come forward.

                    HARRY
He was a weakling. He died!

                    PAUL
              (loves an argument)
Oh! So is it a soldier we've been waiting for?

                    CHUCK
Well, at least a forceful dude who can take
charge of things!

                    PAUL
Ah, perhaps a captain of industry. A business
man. An entrepreneur. Like me! Is that what
the scriptures promised us?

                    HARRY
              (of Paul)
Who is this guy?

                    PAUL
The signs we needed to see in order to
understand that Jesus was the Messiah were
precisely that he was humble, devout and
misunderstood.

                    HARRY
              (struggles)
A loser?

                    PAUL

Exactly!

Now they're all totally confused.

                    PAUL

The last shall be first! And the first last!
Everything is different now!

                    GUS
               (aside to Simon)
We should have turned right back around
and gone home.

                    PAUL

Jesus was God and, and—and he became human.

                    HARRY

What! Make yourself plain, man. You're talking
nonsense!

                    PAUL

He became man… in order to experience the
human condition at its worst… at its… most painful.
Despised, cheated, betrayed! In order… in order…

                    CHUCK

In order to what?

                    PAUL

In order to… to save us from death.

                    HARRY

God?

                    PAUL

Jesus.

                    CHUCK

He died a scoundrel's death, rotting on the
cross with the other criminals!

                    PAUL
You mean the Romans raged and plotted
against him and put him to death with the
connivance of the quisling high priests at
Jerusalem!

Stunned silence. Then the people go wild and attack him. Adam,
Gus, and Simon drag him from the melee within an inch of his
life. The Damascus rabbi finds the letter Paul was given by
Josephus in Jerusalem as it falls to the ground during the scuffle.

020. INTERIOR, DAMASCUS MANSION—DAY

Aretas is the Roman-appointed governor of the region. The rabbi
waits while he reads the letter he found.

                    ARETAS
Jesus Followers. Another Jewish sect?

                    RABBI
They blaspheme.

                    ARETAS
                 (blithely)
Who cares?

                    RABBI
They're seditious.

                    ARETAS
                 (worried)
Oh yeah?

                    RABBI
They believe the end of the world is at hand.

                    ARETAS
But that's only what you Jews are waiting for,
right?

The rabbi hands the letter over and sits.

RABBI
Yes, of course. But not right now.
(of the letter)
Paul seems to have been sent by the Temple
to bring these Jesus Followers back to be
punished. But he's gone over to them instead.

ARETAS
(glances at letter)
And who is this Jesus anyway?

RABBI
Their prophet. He was crucified a year or two
ago in Jerusalem. His brother and his friends have
started a breakaway faction of Judaism centered
around Jesus' teaching. They hold all property in
common, for instance.

ARETAS
Hey, now, that's outright communism!

RABBI
They have no real regard for the authorities,
I'm afraid.

ARETAS
Anti-Roman Jewish patriots, I bet!

RABBI
In a quiet and unassuming sort of way, yes.

ARETAS
Are they popular?

RABBI
No. But they provide a bad example.

ARETAS
(hands back letter)
Okay, here. Find him—this bastard Paul. Kill
him. I haven't got time for this.

021. EXTERIOR, DAMASCUS TRUCK DEPOT—NIGHT

Soldiers are patrolling the quiet streets. Seeing them up ahead, Adam ducks into a side street leading down to where Gus and Simon are overseeing the loading of large crates of commercial goods onto flatbed trucks.

ADAM
(to Gus)
We've got to hurry. They're getting close.

He checks a crate and, as expected, finds Paul inside.

PAUL
Gimme something to eat.

Adam hands him a well-stuffed brown paper lunch bag.

ADAM
Where will you go?

PAUL
East.

ADAM
For how long?

PAUL
I don't know.

They throw ropes around the crate and lift Paul up.

GUS
What about the business, boss?

PAUL
You take over things till you hear from me.
Don't let the contract with the Army lapse.
I've got some thinking to do—things to sort out.
(to Adam)
Adam, thank you.

ADAM

Sorry for all the controversy.

PAUL

Yeah, well—controversy can be useful. Take
it easy. I'll be in touch before long.

And they hoist him out off the loading dock and onto the truck.
The driver shifts into gear and the truck rattles off into the east.

022. INTERIOR, JERUSALEM HOME—DAY

Sheila waits in her kitchen, her children playing beside her, as her
husband, Phillip, finishes a business deal in the street. A new title
card announces: *Jerusalem: 3 Years Later*. Phillip enters.

PHILLIP

We'll save half the money I sold the land for
and the rest we'll give to the community of
believers.

SHEILA

But Phillip, don't you understand that the
community is of one heart and soul now and
that none of us need to own anything privately.
We will share and hold all things in common.

PHILLIP

Yeah, but Sheila, what if things don't work out
the way the apostles say they will?

SHEILA

But they will.

PHILLIP

How can you be so sure?

SHEILA

The Messiah will return and this world will
end as it is written in the scriptures. What need
do we have of our possessions?

KIDS

Yeah, Dad, come on! Get with it!

PHILLIP

Yeah, of course, you're right. Go on ahead
and find the others. I'll be there soon.

Sheila takes the kids outside. Phillip watches her go then stashes
half his cash in a box beneath the table.

023. INTERIOR, JERUSALEM APOSTLE HQ—DAY

Phillip arrives and greets his fellow believers. The man in charge,
Peter, is seated on an overturned box, counting money the various
believers are bringing in and placing before him. He glances over
as Phillip appears, smiling meekly, and places down his cash.
Peter looks at it, pauses, then lifts the stack of hundreds.

PETER
(skeptical)

Are you telling me this is all you got for selling
your farm?

PHILLIP

Yes.

PETER

Come off it.

PHILLIP
(offended)

It is!

PETER

Then you've been taken for a ride, my friend.

PHILLIP

I'm not a good negotiator.

PETER

I think you're holding out on us.

                    PHILLIP
You son of a bitch! How dare you accuse me
of... of... What? What are you suggesting!

The others stop and look on as Peter stubs out his cigarette and
leans forward.

                    PETER
Listen, you have not lied to us, but to God.

                    PHILLIP
Why I oughta—you're nothing but a common
thug yourself! You... You...

Phillip clutches his heart, stutters, and falls to the floor—dead.
Peter drops his cigarette and stands, genuinely spooked.

                    PETER
Wow.
          (then)
Take him out and bury him. Find his wife.
Joseph, come here a minute.

Phillip is taken away and Peter leads Joseph outside.

024. EXTERIOR, JERUSALEM APOSTLE HQ—DAY

Clearing his head, still shook up, Peter gets back to business.

                    PETER
Listen, I need you to go to Cappadocia.

                    JOSEPH
          (surprised)
Now?

                    PETER
Yeah.

                    JOSEPH
Why?

PETER

There's a man there named Paul—I'm not
sure—the tentmaker from Tarsus who
disappeared three years ago. They say he's
out there preaching in Jesus' name.

JOSEPH

Hallelujah.

PETER

Yeah, sure, but who is this guy? Where's he
come off preaching the gospel? He isn't one
of us. He didn't even know Jesus. Find out
who he is. Make friends with him. See what
he knows. How he works. We could use a
good man further afield. But we don't want
no troublemakers. Go on. Get going.

025. INTERIOR, JERUSALEM WAREHOUSE—DAY

Gus is overseeing the loading and unloading of the company's
trucks, signing bills of lading, and checking inventories. Joseph
follows along.

GUS

Cappadocia?

JOSEPH

Yes.

GUS

Whcn?

JOSEPH

Two months ago. Some of our friends heard
him preaching there. I've been sent to go find
him. The leadership of the Way here in
Jerusalem want a meeting.

GUS

The Way?

JOSEPH

That's what we call our movement now.

GUS

Oh boy. Now it's a movement!
                (counts out some money)
If you find him, I think he'll need some cash.
Tell him things here are good.

026. EXTERIOR, CAPPADOCIA SYNAGOGUE—DAY

An angry mob kicks Paul out the door and sends him tumbling down the steps and into the muddy street. A title card announces: *Cappadocia, 36 Common Era.* The local rabbi rushes out to restore order and help Paul to his feet.

RABBI

What's your name?

PAUL

Paul.

RABBI

You're spreading ridiculous rumors and
confusing these people.

PAUL

I'm spreading the good news that has been
revealed to me.

RABBI

By who?

PAUL

By Jesus.

RABBI

And who's he?

PAUL

The Messiah.

The mob starts throwing stones and vegetables at him again until
the rabbi forces them to cut it out.

                    RABBI
         Paul, that's insane. The Messiah is to be the
         savior of our people. Everyone everywhere
         would have heard of him. The situation as it
         now is wouldn't exist. The Messianic Age
         would be at hand.

                    PAUL
         I understand. Listen, Rabbi, I can explain
         everything.

                    RABBI
              (sighs)
         Of course.

                    PAUL
         No really.

                    RABBI
         I'm sure you can! That's the problem with mad
         men like you. Here, go on your way and keep
         out of trouble.

Paul is left there in the street as the rabbi ushers everyone back
inside. There are seven or eight stragglers who linger, curious
about Paul, but bashful. Adam is still with him. And now Joseph
is there too, standing a little farther away. Paul dusts himself off,
picks up his stuff, and glances around at them.

                    PAUL
         Who's with me?

They all just shrug, ambivalent. No one wants to be the first to say
anything.

                    PAUL
              (resigned)
         Okay. Come on.

027. EXTERIOR, CAPPADOCIA RIVER—DAY

Paul kneels at the river's edge, daubing his cuts and bruises with a rag. Eventually, he can't help but notice Joseph lingering nearby.

> PAUL
> And who are you?

> JOSEPH
> I've come from Jerusalem.

> PAUL
> *(unimpressed)*
> Is that so.

> JOSEPH
> I was sent by James, the brother of Jesus—
> and Peter too.

Now Paul is alarmed. He drops his rag and stands back, waiting for more. Joseph comes forward with the money.

> JOSEPH
> And your friend, Gus—he wanted me to bring
> you this money.

Paul hesitates but then takes the money. He pulls Adam aside.

> PAUL
> What do you make of that?

> ADAM
> They are the people who knew Jesus best. We
> could learn a lot from them, maybe.

> PAUL
> *(suspicious)*
> Yeah, maybe.

> JOSEPH
> They've heard of your work and are pleased.

PAUL
(counts the money)
You don't say.

028. EXTERIOR, CAPPADOCIA HIGHWAY—DAY

Paul stomps along the edge of the highway back to Jerusalem. Joseph follows behind with Adam and the stragglers. But then Paul stops and turns. They all skid to a halt.

PAUL
This ain't some sort of a trap, is it?

JOSEPH
Excuse me?

PAUL
An ambush.

JOSEPH
I don't understand.

PAUL
I used to hunt down you followers of the Way and drag you back to the Temple to be condemned as blasphemers and political agitators and whatnot. They used to pay me for it.

JOSEPH
There are a lot of people who think it blasphemous to say Jesus is the Messiah. You wouldn't have been the only one to mistrust us.

Paul comes closer and studies his own hand clenched into a fist, deeply troubled.

PAUL
But I helped. I helped torture him. I helped track him down. I nailed him to the cross.

Joseph hesitates but glances at Adam, who looks down and away. Finally, he approaches carefully and touches Paul's arm.

JOSEPH
Paul, you know that isn't true. You weren't there.

PAUL
(looks right at him)
So what? I could have been.

Then he turns and continues on.

029. INTERIOR, JERUSALEM APOSTLE HQ—DAY

Paul is seated with James, Peter, and John. James is intelligent, patient, and generous. Peter is a street-fighting man. John is a suspicious, older lawyer.

JAMES
Paul, what do you think you're doing exactly?

PAUL
I'm preaching the good news of your brother's teaching—the gospel of the one true God.

PETER
And who gave you permission to do this?

PAUL
Do I need permission?

PETER
Jesus selected us twelve to preach the word.

PAUL
As far as I can tell, you have not been very successful.

PETER
And you have?

                         PAUL
Amongst the Gentiles, yeah. With the Jews,
it's harder.

                        JAMES
                     (surprised)
The Gentiles?

                        PETER
You're preaching to the Gentiles?

                         PAUL
Jesus proclaimed that the final days were at
hand.
                     (to James)
Am I right?

                        JAMES
That's true.

                         PAUL
And in the final days, as it says in the
scriptures, the Gentiles will come to worship
the God of Israel.

                        JAMES
                      (consults)
John?

                         JOHN
              (nods, noncommittal)
Yes.

                         PAUL
In fact, it is a prerequisite for the coming of
the new age.

                         JOHN
                    (points out)
First Israel must be restored, then the Gentiles
will come in.

PAUL

I know, but the enthusiasm of the Gentiles for
the God of Israel makes the Jews take notice.

JOHN

So, you're aiming to make the Jews jealous of
their own heritage?

PAUL

Why not? If it helps restore Israel, why not?

They all consider this. John and Peter are still suspicious. James is
more open-minded.

JAMES

The issue, though, is: are the Gentiles to enter
the community of faith as Gentiles or as Jews?

PETER

Yes, these groups of yours in Damascus,
Cappadocia, Antioch and so on; are the men
circumcised? Do they follow the dietary laws?
Do they observe the Sabbath?

PAUL

Some of them.

PETER
(scoffs)
Some of them?

PAUL

Anyway, I don't really see as how that's so
important.

JOHN

It's what distinguishes us as Jews!

PAUL

No, what distinguishes us as Jews is our belief
in one god and the moral standard that follows

from it. It doesn't say anything in the scriptures
about the Gentiles coming in *as Jews*.

Peter is furious but contains himself and looks at James. James is
impressed with Paul but doesn't want to flatter him.

                    JAMES
Fair enough, Paul. We could be doing better.
Perhaps we're not very well organized.

                    PAUL
Oh, I'm organized. Really, I am. I've run
this tentmaking business for going on fifteen
years now; thirty sometimes forty men on the
payroll; travel, communication, accounting.
Infrastructure. That's the thing, James:
infrastructure. You've gotta have a good
network.

                    JAMES
Infrastructure.

                    PAUL
Exactly. I speak Greek. I know some Latin.
And I've got business contacts all over the
place—all the way up past Macedonia.

                    JAMES
We'll have to think about this. In the meantime,
I think you should continue to preach to the
Gentiles; bring them in without making them
convert by accepting circumcision.

Peter bristles at this. John comes forward and adds—

                    JOHN
But, as it is written: The Gentiles will come to
Mount Zion bearing offerings.

                    JAMES
That's the point.

                         PAUL
You mean donations.

                         JAMES
Yes. Like you say, we here at Jerusalem can
use a bit more infrastructure.

Paul is eager and ready to go—thankful.

                         PAUL
James! Say no more. I'm your man.

030. EXTERIOR, JERUSALEM STREET—DAY

Adam, Joseph, and the stragglers follow Paul as he comes away
from the meeting. Turning into a side street they meet Mitch, a
man about Paul's age.

                         MITCH
Paul, you are deceiving the Gentiles. Jesus,
had you known him, would never have
approved.

                         PAUL
You never knew Jesus either.

                         MITCH
But I live now with the men and women from
Galilee—with the Apostles—and I have Jesus'
teaching directly from them.
               (follows as Paul moves on)
He did not preach to the Gentiles, but sought
only to restore the house of Israel. He referred
to the Gentiles as dogs.

                         PAUL
               (stops and turns)
Yeah, when?

                         MITCH
Once. I forget where exactly.

His point proven, Paul walks on.

                    PAUL
Six, seven, eight years ago you had no time
for God. Remember? I wasted my breath
trying to convince you to be a good Jew and
follow the law.

                    MITCH
Well, things are different now.

                    PAUL
You can say that again.

                    MITCH
Jesus *appeared* to them.

                    PAUL
          (stops again and turns)
To who?

                    MITCH
The Twelve. The Apostles.

Paul backs Mitch up against a wall.

                    PAUL
After he was dead?

                    MITCH
Yeah.

                    PAUL
After they buried him?

                    MITCH
Yeah.

031. INTERIOR, JERUSALEM LIBRARY—DAY

Mitch leads the way into the foyer. Paul stops and thinks.

                              PAUL
          Adam, you wait here. Joseph, go tell Gus and
          Simon to meet us at the hotel.

They run off and Paul follows Mitch up into the library.

032. INTERIOR, JERUSALEM LIBRARY—DAY

Paul and Mitch sit down across from Matthew, a busy historian
bent over his books.

                              MITCH
          Matthew, this is Paul.

                            MATTHEW
                        (keeps working)
          How do you do.

                              PAUL
          Fine. Thanks. Look, can I ask you something?

Matthew leans up from his books and lowers his reading glasses.

                            MATTHEW
          You still work for the Temple rounding up
          us blasphemers and dragging us back to be
          killed?

Paul allows this. He looks aside and bites his lip.

                              MITCH
          Look, Matthew, Paul is one of us now.

                            MATTHEW
                         (skeptical)
          Oh, really.

                              MITCH
          He just came from James and Peter and they
          gave him the thumbs-up to go preach in Jesus'
          name. To the Gentiles!

Matthew is intrigued, but wary.

                    PAUL
          What happened when Jesus appeared to you?

                    MATTHEW
               (taken off guard)
          What?

                    PAUL
          Word on the street is Jesus appeared to you
          all after his death. What was it like? How did
          it happen? What exactly occurred?

Matthew looks to Mitch, and Paul does too.

                    PAUL
          Mitch, scram.

Mitch gets up and leaves. Paul returns to Matthew.

                    MATTHEW
               (slippery)
          Well, it was—it's hard to say.

                    PAUL
          Did it all happen at once? Were you all
          together?

                    MATTHEW
          No. It was more like a private thing. Each of
          us had his own experience, his own revelation.

                    PAUL
          But you saw him?

                    MATTHEW
          In a manner of speaking.

                    PAUL
          Physically?

MATTHEW
Not like a dead man come to life again, no.

PAUL
Then like a ghost?

MATTHEW
No, it was—it's difficult to put into words.

Paul sits back. He eases off, satisfied.

PAUL
Don't sweat it. I know what you mean.

MATTHEW
(suspicious)
What are you saying?

PAUL
I'm saying I know how hard it is to describe
a mystical experience in ordinary language.

MATTHEW
Are you saying it happened to you too?

PAUL
I think so.

MATTHEW
Jesus appeared to you?

PAUL
Something happened to me. I witnessed things
that cannot be said, that defy description, but
the truth of which I comprehend perfectly.

Matthew watches as Paul stands and walks away.

033. EXTERIOR, JERUSALEM HIGHWAY—DAY

Paul's three trucks pull in off the highway. He climbs down from the lead truck, sorting through a stack of letters. Adam, Joseph, Gus, and Simon gather around.

                    PAUL
          It's no small thing what we accomplished back
          there, gentlemen. Having the Jerusalem group's
          okay will open a lot of doors for us.

                    ADAM
          I hope so.

                    PAUL
          Joseph and me will be in Galatia by the end
          of the month. Adam, you head on to Antioch
          with Simon and pass these letters on to our
          friends. Gus, you go all the way to Smyrna,
          unload that cargo, give this letter to our people
          there, then meet up with us in Miletus in the
          spring.

                    GUS
          Right.

                    PAUL
          Okay. God go with you. And get receipts for
          everything.

They all head back to their trucks, climb up into them, and rumble off into the distance.

034. EXTERIOR, LYSTRA SYNAGOGUE—DAY

Paul gets tossed out of the synagogue and lands in the dirt beside Joseph. Title card: *Lystra, Somewhere in Anatolia, Months Later.* The local rabbi stands in the doorway, shakes his head, and points the way out of town. Paul picks himself up, takes his bag from Joseph, and the two of them hobble off down the street.

035. EXTERIOR, LYSTRA MARKETPLACE—DAY

Coming up the street, Paul spots an apparently lame beggar lying on a blanket, pleading for alms. He stops.

BEGGAR

Please, alms!

PAUL

How long have you been this way?

BEGGAR

Always.

Paul thinks a moment and looks around at the marketplace confusion. He hands his bag to Joseph.

JOSEPH

What are you doing?

PAUL

There are some miracles that need performing.
Wait here.

Paul comes down beside the beggar and drops a few small coins in his bowl. As the beggar is inspecting the amount he has received, Paul lays his hand on the man's shoulder. The beggar looks at him, startled. Paul looks him straight in the eye and smiles beatifically while digging his finger deep in behind the man's collar bone. The beggar begins to rise to his feet in too much pain to even speak, fluttering his eyelids up into the sunlight. Paul watches his patient mercifully as he lifts the man's entire weight in his iron grip.

BEGGAR

(in pain)

Ahhh!!!!!

People look on, amazed. Joseph expects the worst. Finally, the beggar is standing on his own two feet. Paul steps back and raises his arms to heaven.

PAUL

Praise be to the Lord!

The crowd goes wild. The beggar, having no choice, plays along. He falls to his knees, worshiping Paul.

                    BEGGAR
          The great god Zeus has come down in human
          form!

                    CROWD
               (cheers)
          Zeus! Zeus!

The crowd rushes forward to touch Paul. But Paul scowls down at the beggar.

                    PAUL
          Not Zeus! Jesus! Jesus!

Swatting away the outstretched hands of his new fans, Paul tries to locate Joseph, who is being tossed about in the excited crowd.

                    CROWD
          Zeus! Zeus!

036. EXTERIOR, LYSTRA SIDE STREETS—DAY

Paul drags Joseph along by the sleeve as he tries to escape the hysterical mob. He makes a turn into another street and stops before a procession of Greek priests of Zeus with a group of oxen adorned with garlands. The crowd settles down but whispers excitedly amongst themselves.

                    PRIEST OF ZEUS
               (falls to his knees)
          Divine source of all amazement, Immortal
          Zeus, we offer sacrifice of these oxen in your
          honor.

                    PAUL
          Friends, why are you doing this?
               (when the priest looks up)
          Me and my friend here are mortal just like you.

PRIEST OF ZEUS
(stands)
But you cure the lame.

Paul frowns and looks back over his shoulder to the beggar, who
fades back into the crowd, hiding. Paul returns to the priest and
makes the most of things.

PAUL
It is not I who do anything, but God through
me. In fact, it might be said, that the lame
man begging for alms in the street discovered
within himself the power of the one true
living God.

The beggar considers this and nods, impressed. He'll use it as his
own sometime. Meanwhile—

PRIEST OF ZEUS
What god is this?

PAUL
The only god. The god who made the heaven
and the earth and the sea and all that is in
them.

PRIEST OF ZEUS
Ah, so you are a magician of the Jewish faith.

PAUL
Jewish, yes, but not a magician.

PRIEST OF ZEUS
Then how do you explain what you have done?

PAUL
Faith.

PRIEST OF ZEUS
(trying hard)
Knowledge.

PAUL

No.

PRIEST OF ZEUS

I'm confused.

PAUL

Don't be. I can explain everything.

The priest of Zeus sees someone approaching. Paul follows his gaze and sees the local rabbi.

PAUL
(under his breath)

Shit!

JOSEPH

It's the rabbi.

PAUL

And his posse.

The rabbi arrives with his angry followers. He frowns at Paul.

037. EXTERIOR, LYSTRA CITY GATE—DAY

Paul stumbles from the city gate, badly bruised and beaten, as the populace continues to pelt him with stones. He collapses and lies unconscious in the dirt. The crowd wanders away, leaving him for dead. Joseph approaches warily, afraid for the worst. He reaches down and tugs at Paul's arm, causing him to roll over a little onto his back. He moans. Joseph steps back, startled, and bumps into a local teenager.

TIMOTHY

Come on, I'll help you. We can carry him
to the garage.

038. EXTERIOR, LYSTRA YARD—DAY

Timothy has got them to a safe place behind an auto parts garage

and assists as Joseph tends to Paul's wounds. Joseph sees writing
utensils.

JOSEPH
Are you a scribe?

TIMOTHY
Yeah. Here, this is clean water.

JOSEPH
(helping Paul drink)
Are you a Jew?

TIMOTHY
No. Greek. But I love this one god idea.
Great—really modern—everyone's talking
about it.

PAUL
(weakly)
We could use a scribe.

He coughs up blood, moans, and passes out again.

TIMOTHY
Is he going to be okay?

JOSEPH
(drinks, then)
It'll take more than an angry mob to kill this
man. Believe me.

TIMOTHY
I heard people talking about him in
Thessalonica.

JOSEPH
What were you doing in Thessalonica?

TIMOTHY
My master had business there.

JOSEPH

You're a slave, then.

TIMOTHY
(proudly)
Yeah. And I have the rights of a slave too.

JOSEPH

You'd have to give all that up to come
along with us.

TIMOTHY

The way I see it: the future is this one god
of Israel thing. Staying here, even with all
the benefits of being a slave, I'm afraid I'll
stagnate. I need adventure. New challenges.
Intellectually, I mean. I want to be out there
on the cutting edge of culture. Get me?

039. EXTERIOR, STREET—DAY

Paul and his men are in a huge brawl. They escape but are chased
through the streets.

040. EXTERIOR, FIELD—DAY

Paul and his small gang run across a field. People are firing guns
at them.

041. EXTERIOR, JUNK YARD—NIGHT

Timothy is dejected, sitting at a writing table with his head hung
low.

PAUL
(shakes his head)
So, what did you think it'd be like! Wine,
women and song all the live long day!
Intellectual adventure! I'll give you
intellectual adventure. This world is about to
end, my son. Think about that!

TIMOTHY
(sniffles)
Should I write that down?

PAUL
Bet your ass you write that down. But not yet.
I'm working on it still. What's that?

TIMOTHY
(hands him a letter)
From Jerusalem, from Peter.

PAUL
(reads, sighs)
He's heard my core group now includes
a Gentile.
(to Joseph)
Should I worry about this?

JOSEPH
It's always going to be an issue with those
guys.

TIMOTHY
(scared)
Do I have to get, you know, circumcised?

PAUL
Relax. Let's finish this letter to the Corinthians.
Where were we?

TIMOTHY
(reads)
"Even as the testimony of Christ was confirmed
in you—"

PAUL
Right.
(dictates as Timothy writes)
Even as the testimony of Christ was
confirmed in you… So that you come behind

in no gift, waiting for the coming of our Lord
Jesus Christ, who shall also confirm you until
the end, so that you may be blameless.

041. INTERIOR, CORINTH HALL—DAY

A small group of followers listen as an older man, Jonas, reads
Paul's letter aloud. A title card announces: *Corinth*.

> JONAS
> *(with difficulty)*
> "So that you come behind in no gift; waiting
> for the coming of our Lord Jesus Christ: who
> shall also confirm you until the end, so that
> you may be blameless in the day of our Lord
> Jesus Christ."

No one understands what Paul's letter is saying. But a young man,
David, stands and asks—

> DAVID
> Excuse me, Jonas, can you read that other
> part again—the part about foolishness and
> wisdom?

Everyone agrees, eager for further clarification. Jonas finds the
passage while David glances back across the room to Rachel, a
beautiful, lively widow of thirty-five dressed in mourning and
standing just inside the door.

> JONAS
> *(reads)*
> "For the preaching of the cross is to those that
> perish thought to be foolishness. But to us,
> who are saved (and do not perish), it is the
> power of God. For it is written, I will destroy
> the wisdom of the wise and will bring to
> nothing the understanding of the prudent."

He lowers the letter and thinks this over. David thinks it over too
and repeats softly—

DAVID

"That you may be blameless in the day of our
Lord Jesus Christ."

042. EXTERIOR, CORINTH STREET—DAY

David comes outside with the others and crosses the square to
where Rachel is waiting. She is nervous but starts to glow when
she sees him. They speak as they move through the streets. They
try mighty hard but cannot conceal their desire for one another.

DAVID

Well, the idea seems to be this: we are a new
creation.

RACHEL
(uncertain what he means)
A new creation?

DAVID

Just by having faith in the return of the
Christ, we are no longer beholden to the laws
and customs.

RACHEL

That makes us sound like criminals.

DAVID

No. We have to be good. But what good is
there in not loving.

RACHEL

I understand that much. To love is the whole
of the law. Or something like that. Right?

DAVID

We are told to live in the spirit. Old relation-
ships, one to another, are passed away. They
are just words. It's our relationship now to
God that defines our relationship to each
other.

                              RACHEL
So, it's okay for me, a widow, to be in love
with my stepson?

                              DAVID
All these distinctions are meaningless now.

After glancing around to make sure they're alone, David guides
her back into an alcove. They kiss passionately as a new title card
announces: *Meanwhile, in Philippi.*

043. EXTERIOR, PHILIPPI FACTORY—DAY

Paul and Timothy come up the road and encounter a number of
women exiting work at a textile factory.

                              PAUL
Can you please tell me where the local
synagogue is?

                              LYDIA
Your young friend here is tired and thirsty,
I think.

Timothy sits on the ground and Lydia brings him some water.

                              TIMOTHY
Thank you.

                              LYDIA
                            (to Paul)
You're Paul, the Apostle to the Gentiles.

                              PAUL
Well, technically, I'm not an apostle, apparently.
But, if no one else will do the work, what am I
supposed to do about it?

                              LYDIA
I heard you speak in Philadelphia in the spring.
They beat you with sticks.

                              PAUL
They broke my arm. It'll never be perfectly
straight again, I think. Look at that. Were you
baptized?

                              LYDIA
No.

                              PAUL
What are you waiting for?

                              LYDIA
                    (shrugs, looks away)
The synagogue is on the far side of the city.

                              PAUL
Damn. I thought so.

                              LYDIA
It's late. You and your helper can stay at my
house. We're going back now anyway.

Paul and Timothy follow the women and Timothy runs a little
ahead to catch up with Lydia.

                            TIMOTHY
Maybe you shouldn't introduce us to anyone.

                              LYDIA
Why, are you ashamed of yourselves?

                            TIMOTHY
No, but wherever my boss goes, there's usually
a riot or something. Things get broken.

Lydia laughs and moves along. Timothy hangs back and Paul
catches up with him.

                              PAUL
Stop flirting with her, you punk. She's a
married woman.

044. EXTERIOR, PHILIPPI, LYDIA'S HOUSE—DAY

Lydia leads everyone into the yard of the house and finds her husband, Ben, a mechanic, looking up from under the hood of a car.

> LYDIA
> This is Paul, the Apostle to the Gentiles, and his scribe, Timothy. They'll sleep in the garage tonight. They've walked all day.

> BEN
> Okay. But, please, no trouble.

> PAUL
> I only need to sleep.

> BEN
> I saw them try to kill you last winter when you spoke in Iconium.

> LYDIA
> They broke his arm in Philadelphia.
> *(to Paul)*
> Show him.

But before Paul can, they all look over at a mad-eyed girl out in the street, pointing at them, her eyes rolling back in her head.

> ESMERALDA
> These men are slaves of the most-high God who proclaim to you a way of salvation! These men are slaves of the most-high God who proclaim to you a way of salvation!

Timothy hides behind Paul, frightened.

> PAUL
> What's wrong with her?

> LYDIA
> She's the neighbor's slave. She has psychic

powers and makes her owners a lot of money
by fortune-telling.

PAUL
(throws down his bag)
That's sick.

He walks up to Esmeralda and holds her by the chin, forcing her
to look right at him. She is startled. Her eyes come normal again.

PAUL
Stop this madness, child. By the power of
Jesus, you are now free from this evil.
Now, beat it.

He lets go of her and she jumps back, shocked. Paul returns to
Lydia's garage and the girl runs away.

045. EXTERIOR, PHILIPPI, LYDIA'S HOUSE—DAY

The next morning, Lydia and Ben run into the yard just as a gang
of their neighbors rush in and seize Paul and Timothy, dragging
them out into the street.

046. EXTERIOR, PHILIPPI MARKETPLACE—DAY

The mob drags Paul and his sidekick up before the town's magistrate who, accompanied by his entourage, is shopping for vegetables.

NEIGHBOR
(rehearsed)
These men are disturbing our city! They are
Jews and are advocating customs that are not
lawful for us as Romans to adopt or observe!

MAGISTRATE
(amused)
Neighbor, I know you from the marketplace.
You are incapable of formulating a statement
such as this on your own. What is this all about?

WIFE
These men terrorized our slave and now she's
no good to us anymore!

Esmeralda starts crying and throws herself at her mistress' feet.
The wife kicks her away and the girl whimpers there on the pavement.

MAGISTRATE
Is not this the fortune-teller, then?

WIFE
She's lost her powers, sir! He drove them out
of her!

MAGISTRATE
Have you been mistreated, young woman?

Esmeralda is on the spot and doesn't know what to say. Her owners glare at her.

ESMERALDA
(recites weakly)
These men are slaves of the most-high God
who proclaim to you a way of salvation.

MAGISTRATE
Ah! Jews proclaiming a way of salvation.
Well, that's not very unusual.
(to Paul)
What's your name? Where do you come from?

PAUL
Saul of Tarsus called Paul, recently of Jerusalem,
Damascus, Antioch, etcetera.

MAGISTRATE
And what did you do to her?

PAUL
She was possessed of an unclean spirit.

MAGISTRATE
Of course! That's how she makes her living.
I myself have paid her to tell me the future.

PAUL
Why?

MAGISTRATE
How else am I to govern this mob! Her foresight
is indispensable.

PAUL
She's a terrorized maniac. She'd say anything
to anyone to keep from being whipped.

NEIGHBOR
Now that's unfair. She's talented. Everyone
says so. She predicted the solar eclipse last
year.

Impressed, the magistrate looks at Paul, daring him to refute this.
Paul looks at Timothy.

TIMOTHY
The Arabs can all do that. They say it's like
clockwork.

Paul returns to the magistrate, addressing everyone.

PAUL
There's no need to be possessed of a demon
to be able to predict an eclipse. If this slave
girl is smart enough to know such things,
she ought to be taught to read and write. She
ought to be freed.

The crowd murmurs its disapproval.

MAGISTRATE
Easy there, pal. No need to threaten the very
foundation of our economy.

PAUL
(to Esmeralda)
You know in your heart what's right and true.

A member of the entourage whispers to the magistrate, showing him a newspaper article and pointing to Paul.

MAGISTRATE
Ah, Paul—the Apostle to the Gentiles.

PAUL
That's not… well, technically… okay.

MAGISTRATE
You caused a good deal of havoc in Pergamum,
it says here.

PAUL
That was three years ago.

MAGISTRATE
(to his entourage)
Throw these two men into jail and keep them
secure until further notice.

Moments later, the crowd sings and dances, following the soldier, Anthony, who drags Paul and Timothy off to jail.

047. INTERIOR, PHILIPPI JAIL—DAY

Paul and Timothy are in shackles attached to chains anchored in the brick wall and Timothy's are too tight.

TIMOTHY
It hurts.

PAUL
No, it doesn't.

TIMOTHY
Boss, I'm sorry. It does.

                    PAUL
This is all an illusion.

                  TIMOTHY
The chains?

                    PAUL
Yes. The chains, the walls, the air we breathe.
Reality. All of it. If you can remember that,
the pain is trivial.

The soldier, Anthony, hears all this. He's interested.

                  ANTHONY
If none of this is real, what is real?

                    PAUL
Christ's kingdom.

                  ANTHONY
And where is that?

                    PAUL
Right here.

                  ANTHONY
But I thought this, right here, is not real.

                    PAUL
It isn't. You've got to look beyond it. There
is more than one plane of being. This, reality,
what we call reality, is only one, the lowest
plane of being. Understand?

The poor soldier does not. But he'd like to. He looks up and down
the hall to make sure the coast is clear, then enters the cell and
loosens the shackles on their ankles and wrists.

                  TIMOTHY
                 (relieved)
Bless you, friend.

Then they stop and look around. There's a deep rumbling. The ground is trembling. Anthony jumps up to look outside. The walls around them begin to shake and most of the building collapses. A title card appears: *Earthquake*. Once the dust settles, Paul and Timothy get to their feet. Cries are heard down the hall, screaming in the streets outside. Anthony staggers up from under the rubble, throws off his helmet, and looks at Paul in awe.

                    ANTHONY
          Did you do that?

                    PAUL
          What?

                    ANTHONY
          You, Jewish magician, did your Jesus Christ
          cause that to happen?

                    PAUL
               (standing)
          Knock it off. Pull yourself together. That was
          an earthquake!

Timothy tugs at his chains and they fall easily from their moorings in the wall. He looks out into the street.

                    TIMOTHY
          That whole side of the street is destroyed.

                    PAUL
               (to Anthony)
          Go see to your associates down the hall.

Anthony moves off. A crowd of other, happy, convicts scramble past, escaping.

                    CONVICT
          Come on! Let's get outta here!

Timothy is anxious to join them, but Paul holds him back and gestures that they should wait. Anthony returns, worried.

ANTHONY
They're all dead. The prisoners have escaped.

He raises his sword to kill himself.

PAUL
Wait! Stop!

ANTHONY
The magistrate will make me kill myself,
anyway, for failing in my duty.

PAUL
What failure? Here we are, still in chains. We
were your responsibility, not those other slobs,
perverts, and pickpockets.

TIMOTHY
The magistrate told you to keep us, my master
and I, secure until further notice.

PAUL
I would say you've done your duty excellently
and will testify on your behalf if the magistrate
insists.

ANTHONY
(falls to his knees)
What must I do to join the people of the Way?

PAUL
Believe in the Lord Jesus.

ANTHONY
What am I supposed to believe? Tell me, and
I will.

PAUL
I'll explain all that later. Right now, go tell
the magistrate what happened and that we
are still in custody.

ANTHONY

You won't escape?

PAUL

No.

Anthony gets up and runs off.

TIMOTHY

I question your sanity sometimes.

PAUL

Me too.

TIMOTHY

Have you no concern for your own
self-preservation?

PAUL

"When in Rome, do as the Romans do."

TIMOTHY

This is not Rome.

PAUL

That's what you think. Everything is Rome
these days. It's a state of mind!

TIMOTHY

The Romans slaughter criminals in the arena
as an idle pastime.

PAUL

Okay, don't do everything the Romans do.
But, still, there are the laws—Roman laws.
What's the point in you and I being fugitives
when the whole point of our travels is to
make known the ways of the Lord? We can't
do that in secret. We can't do that in prison.

Timothy gives up and lies down in the corner. He goes to sleep.

048. INTERIOR, PHILIPPI JAIL—DAY

Anthony returns while other soldiers clear debris and carry away
dead bodies.

ANTHONY
The magistrate sends word to let you go.
Come out now and go in peace.

He unfastens the shackles. Timothy is up in a flash and ready to
go. Paul sits and thinks. Anthony and Timothy stop in the doorway, look back and wait for him.

PAUL
They have beaten me in public, uncondemned,
a Roman citizen, and have thrown me into
prison. And now they are going to discharge
me in secret?
(stands)
Certainly not! Let them come and take me out
themselves!

Timothy shakes his head in dismay. Anthony looks between his
two new friends and tries to decide what to do.

PAUL
Go on. Tell them.

TIMOTHY
This is madness!

PAUL
We have to be seen to be legitimate.

TIMOTHY
But to the Romans? I thought you wanted to
be understood by your fellow Jews?

PAUL
I am a Jew and a Roman citizen. Why should
one disqualify the other? Convincing the

Romans of Christ Jesus is just as important
as convincing the Jews.

049. INTERIOR, MAGISTRATE'S OFFICE—DAY

Having just delivered his message, Anthony stands before the
magistrate and his advisers.

                    MAGISTRATE
          (pained)
     A Roman citizen?

                    ANTHONY
     Yes, sir.

                    ADVISOR
     Perhaps the man merely requires an apology.

                    MAGISTRATE
     A public apology?

                    ADVISOR
     Obviously—and some gifts.

The magistrate looks aside, sighs, and scratches his head. Then,
bracing himself, he stands.

                    MAGISTRATE
     Okay then. Let's do it.

050. EXTERIOR, PHILIPPI TOWN HALL—DAY

Adam, Gus, and Simon are waiting outside the town hall when
Paul and Timothy are led out the front door. The crowd goes
crazy like Paul's now a rock star. The magistrate and his entourage usher them over to a few brand-new motorcycles and a fancy
little sports car. Paul, ignoring all this, spots Adam and waves him
over.

                    ADAM
     I got here as fast as I could.

PAUL

No sweat. Got the mail? Thanks. Where's
Joseph?

ADAM

He'll meet us in Antioch.

Meanwhile, the magistrate makes his obligatory send-off speech.

MAGISTRATE

Goodbye to our friends Paul and Timothy.
Please consider the gates of our city open to
you and your friends and please accept these
gifts from the city of Philippi.

PAUL

Yeah, AND?

MAGISTRATE
(reluctantly)
Yes, best wishes to our friends, the followers
of Jesus Christ, the Messiah, who alone
forgives sins, etcetera, etcetera.

PAUL

Fair enough! Let's go!

The crowd cheers them on as, elsewhere, Esmeralda struggles
through the crowd with a suitcase.

PAUL
(to Anthony)
So, friend, you with us?

ANTHONY

I'm with you. But I've got to finish out my
tour of duty here in Philippi.

PAUL

Good. Gus, take his information. See you
down the road there, pal!

GUS

What's your name?

ANTHONY

Anthony.

TIMOTHY
(behind the wheel)
Where to now, boss?

PAUL

What do you think, Adam?

Adam straddles one of the motorcycles and has no doubts:

ADAM

Corinth. Big trouble. Our friend David is
living with his stepmother.

PAUL

Gross!!!

ADAM

She's young and beautiful and David's one
of our best people.

PAUL

Shit! Not even the pagans go in for that sort
of thing!

ADAM

Yeah, well, the church in Corinth is about to
blow itself to pieces.

PAUL

Come on!

Simon and Gus jump on their bikes and start their motors. They
form a motorcade and lead the sports car, inch by inch, through
the dense crowd. Esmeralda kicks and punches her way through
the cheering masses, trying to catch up.

051. EXTERIOR, ROAD—DAY

Paul and his gang thunder along on their way to Corinth.

052. INTERIOR, RACHEL'S HOME—DAY

The front door is thrown open. David and Rachel jump up in bed, startled. Paul is on the threshold.

> DAVID
>
> Paul!

> PAUL
>
> Sorry, miss. David—outside.

053. EXTERIOR, RACHEL'S HOME—DAY

David stumbles out into the morning, tucking in his shirt.

> PAUL
>
> What the hell's going on here, David?

> DAVID
>
> We're in love.

> PAUL
>
> She's your father's wife.

> DAVID
>
> But he's dead. And she's closer to my age
> than she ever was to his.

> PAUL
>
> That don't matter. It ain't right!

> DAVID
>
> I thought you said we were new creations.
> That the laws and the customs no longer
> applied to us?

Paul has to think about this.

                    PAUL
Did I? I said that?

David looks at Adam who glances at Timothy, who flips through
some of the letters. He hands one to Paul who holds it up to the
light and quickly scans it.

                    DAVID
                 (adds)
I consulted the spirit within me like you
suggest and—

                    PAUL
                 (concedes)
Okay. Okay. Okay…
                 (aside, to Timothy)
We've gotta rethink all this—terminology.
                 (then, to David)
Can you find someplace for these guys to
wash up and rest?

                    DAVID
Sure. This way.

                    GUS
                 (off)
Oh boy. Boss, you might want to weigh in
on this.

They look over and see Gus standing at the open trunk of the
sports car. Coming around back, they see Esmeralda inside clutching her little suitcase. She watches Paul anxiously. Paul sighs and
turns away.

                    PAUL
Great. Now we're kidnappers too.

                    DAVID
I'll take care of her.

Gus helps Esmeralda out of the trunk and David leads everyone away. Paul hangs back and cocks his thumb at the house.

                         PAUL
              David, what's her name?

                        DAVID
              Rachel.

Paul gestures for them all to get lost and steps up to the door. He
knocks.

                         PAUL
                       (gently)
              Rachel?

                        RACHEL
                  (off, from inside)
              Maniac!

Paul sighs and scratches his head. He tries again.

                         PAUL
              Can I come in?

                        RACHEL
                  (off, calms down)
              Wait a minute.

As he waits, Paul turns back to the street and finds two little kids
watching him.

                         PAUL
              Grace be unto you both and peace from God
              our Father.

                         KID
              Can we have a ride on your motorcycle?

But now Rachel is at the door, holding it open and peeking around
the edge. She gives Paul the once over, considers, then steps
aside. Paul enters.

054. INTERIOR, RACHEL'S HOME—DAY

There's a brief and uneasy standoff in the kitchen before Rachel
finally turns away to the counter.

RACHEL

Coffee?

PAUL
(relieved, sits)

Yes. Thanks.

A new title card: *Feminist Theology*.

RACHEL

I read your letter to the Galatians not so long
ago and there you say to them: "There is neither
male nor female for all are one in Christ Jesus."

PAUL

You're taking that out of context.

RACHEL

Maybe. But it's a great idea. Who is God?

PAUL

The Father.

RACHEL

Why not the mother?

PAUL

Because that's paganism all over again.
Earth Mother silliness. Fecundity. Renewal.
Basically, just a license to be possessive,
brutal, and superstitious.

RACHEL

Okay. Fine. Why any gender at all? I mean,
as long as we're groping for some useful
abstractions.

PAUL

God is not an abstraction.

RACHEL

God is the essential abstraction.

PAUL

He's reality.

RACHEL

Why not then say Reality is God and forget
all the gender identification?

PAUL
(sips coffee)
Hey, don't come at me with all that modernist
critical lingo, sister! You know what I'm
talking about!

RACHEL

Hey! Language is important! It decides how
people take complicated feelings and organize
them into ideas and beliefs. And those ideas
and beliefs then go on to shape culture, the law,
politics, life in the street. You know, I've got
to live in this town.

PAUL

You're complaining about peer group pressure?
Are you kidding me! Try not moving in with
your husband's son!

RACHEL

But I love him. He loves me. I mean it's not
like he is my own child. We're practically the
same age.

PAUL

It sends the wrong message to the community.
Sort of like, you know, anything goes if you're
a follower of Christ.

                    RACHEL
So, you see, personal morality is a social
construct.

                    PAUL
                 (exhausted)
Wow. Okay. You win. I can't argue with you
anymore.

                    RACHEL
Here, get some rest. I gotta go to work.

                    PAUL
Thank you.

                    RACHEL
You know, for what it's worth: though we're
all speaking English and pretending to be
ancient Jews—the Hebrew word used in the
scriptures to denote wife is "*ezer*" which
means help or helper. It's the same word the
scriptures use seventeen times to describe the
kind of help God brings to his people in times
of need. Think about that.

                    PAUL
You're saying God's a girl?

                    RACHEL
             (checks her wristwatch)
Oh shit! I'm late!

She grabs her coat and leaves, slamming the door behind her. Paul
falls back and passes out.

055. INTERIOR, ANTIOCH SYNAGOGUE—DAY

A small crowd listens as Paul and the local rabbi debate.

                    RABBI
My friend, the law is holy and unchangeable.

PAUL

But it is also of universal application. That's
what makes it really holy.

The rabbi and the crowd find this intriguing. They consider it. A
new title card appears: *Antioch.*

PAUL
(continues)
Correct? If we insist there is only one God
then it follows that there is only one mankind.
And God is the God of all mankind. And—

JOSEPH
(intercedes)
And it is to preach this word that we have set
out this far from Jerusalem.

Everyone seems to like this. They relax, nodding, thinking it over.
But Paul is quietly furious.

056. EXTERIOR, ANTIOCH STREET—DAY

Paul and Joseph walk in strained silence. Finally, he mimics:

PAUL
"And it is to preach this word that we have
set out this far from Jerusalem."
(spits)
What the fuck was that!

JOSEPH
I knew where you were headed in there and I
just cannot be beaten up by a crowd of my co-
religionists anymore. Okay?

PAUL
Oh, come on!

JOSEPH
I mean it!

PAUL

All the teachings, all the prophecies, all the
history of Israel preserved in the sacred
writings point to one divine event: the coming
into the world of a Savior.

JOSEPH

Sure.

PAUL

And you agree Jesus was that Savior?

JOSEPH

Yes.

PAUL

And so what now?

JOSEPH

We wait for him to return.

PAUL

No.

JOSEPH

What!

PAUL

We don't wait. We make it happen.
Torah—the law—it's only holding us back.

JOSEPH

You see! You can't say that to a room full of
Jews and expect to go home in one piece!
This is what I'm talking about!

PAUL

Jesus replaces the law.

JOSEPH

Not so loud!

                    PAUL

He is the fulfillment of the law *and* the
negation of the law. Get it?
                    (has a better idea)
No! He negates the law *because* he is its
fulfillment.
                    (pats his pockets)
I gotta write this down.

Joseph is exhausted. He steps aside and sits. Paul watches him.

                  JOSEPH

Oh, man.

                   PAUL

You know it's true. You can feel the rightness
of it.

                  JOSEPH

How far are you going to push this?

                   PAUL

I saw Jesus. He revealed himself to me. Just
like he did to the Jerusalem gang.

Joseph doesn't know what to say to this. Meanwhile, Timothy
runs up.

                 TIMOTHY

Peter is here from Jerusalem. He's in the town
square.

                  JOSEPH
                (despondent)
You see what I mean! Word gets around!

                   PAUL

Ease up. I can deal with Peter.
                (to Timothy)
Go get everyone. Bring them downtown to
the restaurant.

057. INTERIOR, ANTIOCH RESTAURANT—DAY

Paul introduces his converts to Peter.

PAUL
This is Gus, Simon, Timothy our scribe.
Anthony. He was there during the earthquake
in Philippi.

PETER
You're a soldier?

ANTHONY
Yes.

PETER
Where's your squadron?

ANTHONY
We're stationed at Palmyra. I'm on a month's
leave.

PETER
Nice to meet you.

PAUL
This is Esmeralda who hid herself in the trunk
of our car.

ESMARELDA
Hi.

PETER
You've done well. Many good people.
            (of the food laid on the table)
But will these people become Jews themselves?

PAUL
What, you mean, the food? Well, it's not
kosher, it's true. But I'm concerned with
their hearts and minds. Not with their stomachs.

PETER
(grins, undecided)
Maybe you're right. I don't know.

But then James and John enter the restaurant with their own people. They come over to the table and nod hello to everyone. But they go sit across the room. Peter is self-conscious and gets up.

PETER
Excuse me a moment.

Paul watches as Peter crosses over to James and his gang.

JAMES
What are you doing at a table eating with the Gentiles?

PETER
I had to talk with Paul. He introduced me to his converts.

JOHN
But it's not right for a Jew.

PAUL
(calls across the room)
Gentlemen! What's the problem?

JOHN
(calls back)
It's not right for a Jew like yourself to be eating unblessed food.

PAUL
I'm not. I eat kosher, strictly. But our friends here are not Jews.

JOHN
You shouldn't even be at table with your friends.

PAUL

They're your friends too, John. All these
people worship the one true God.

JOHN

Yeah, well, are they circumcised?

PAUL

Of course not. Only us idiots still mutilate
ourselves that way.

Some of the Jerusalem gang stand up, knocking back their chairs.
Cutlery slides to the floor. Paul stands up too and is joined a moment later by his friends. Joseph leaves Paul's table and crosses
over to the Jerusalem faction.

PAUL

Where are you going!

JOSEPH

It's wrong, Paul. You've gone too far.

PAUL

Jerk.

JAMES
(stands)
Okay! Okay. Settle down. Gentlemen, please.

Everyone sits back down. James discreetly gestures to Paul that
they should meet outside.

058. EXTERIOR, ANTIOCH RESTAURANT—DAY

JAMES
(steps outside)
This is becoming a crisis.

PAUL
(follows)
I agree.

JAMES

You do?

PAUL

Yes.

JAMES

What do you suggest we do about it?

PAUL

I don't know what you and your crowd are
going to do about it. But me and my gang are
going to preach the gospel of Jesus Christ,
the Messiah, to anyone we meet to the ends
of the earth.

JAMES

Are you trying to start a new religion?

PAUL

No. I'm just pointing out what seems perfectly
obvious to me in the scriptures in the light of
Jesus' death.

JAMES

It's his *life* we try to remember.

PAUL

And that's where you miss the point entirely.
But don't worry. It's not just you. Everyone
misses this.

JAMES

Everyone misses it because it's your own
private invention.

PAUL

My own private revelation.

JAMES

Look, if we gave credence to this, your own

private revelation, what's to stop some…
(uses a man passing as an example)
…well, some Arab in the desert out there
somewhere 600 years from now from saying
that God speaks to him in a cave somewhere
and delivers a whole new set of laws?

PAUL
If this sick world is still here six hundred
years from now, I would have to consider
that an unbelievable act of kindness on the
part of God.

JAMES
If you want me to believe that Jesus, my
brother, was the Messiah, explain to me why
the prophecies have not been fulfilled.

PAUL
They are being fulfilled—by me. I have been
directed to make these prophecies come true.
To preach to the Gentiles and to the Jews alike.
To the ends of the earth. Only then! Only then
will Jesus return.

JAMES
Paul, you're a difficult man.

PAUL
No. It's a difficult world.

059. EXTERIOR, GALATIA COURTYARD—DAY

Peter is roughing up some of the Galatian church members. He grabs their elder, Apollos, and starts grilling him. A title card reads: *Galatia.*

PETER
When Paul was here, did he say that he
represents the God of Israel and that Jesus is
God's designated Messiah?

APOLLOS
                    (terrified)
Yeah.

PETER
Did he say that Jesus' coming was in accord
with the scriptures, and that scripture reveals
God's will and intention?

APOLLOS
Yeah, well—I guess.

PETER
Do you know that those who accept Jesus as
God's Messiah have committed themselves to
obeying the ordinances of God as revealed to
Israel in scripture?

APOLLOS
I suppose so.

PETER
Have you read Genesis 17 lately?

APOLLOS
Not lately, no.

Peter motions over one of his people, Ira, a lawyer, to explain the
scriptures, which he opens and points to.

IRA
                    (high-speed legalese)
Genesis 17 expressly stipulates that all
descendants of Abraham, that is, all males
who follow the ordinances of the God of
Israel, are to be circumcised. Further, it clearly
says that those who are not circumcised will
be cut off from membership in the covenant
between God, Abraham, and his descendants.

They stand back, their point proven, and challenge the old man to respond. But Apollos has no idea what they're talking about.

060. INTERIOR, THESSALONICA ROOMS—DAY

Paul reads the letter from the Galatians.

                         PAUL
     Those bastards!

                       TIMOTHY
     It seems to be true, though. The scriptures do
     say—

                         PAUL
     Shut up!
                       (stops, sighs)
     Sorry. Look, we gotta respond in the same
     way. We gotta quote scripture too and prove
     our point.

                       TIMOTHY
                     (sarcastic)
     The *point* being?

                         PAUL
     You Gentiles must not be circumcised. That's
     idolatry! You must come to the worship of
     God as Gentiles.

                       TIMOTHY
     But that is not what the scriptures say.

                         PAUL
     Don't tell me what the scriptures say. I know
     the scriptures backwards and forwards.

                       TIMOTHY
     Well, then, what do they say?

                         PAUL
     They say all sorts of things.

Timothy folds his arms and shakes his head. Paul turns away to the window, thinking. A new title card announces: *Thessalonica: Biblical Exegesis (the invention of)*.

PAUL

We'll have to start at the beginning, with Abraham, God's promise to Abraham.

TIMOTHY
(sarcastic)

For instance, Genesis 17 where God commands him and all his male descendants to be circumcised?

PAUL
(optimistic)

Exactly! We'll ignore that chapter completely and go directly to God's initial call to Abraham. Come on, get your pen.

Timothy does and leans over his desk.

PAUL
(musing)

"Descendant of Abraham…"

TIMOTHY

Should I write that?

PAUL

No. "Abraham had faith in God and he reckoned it to him as righteousness."

TIMOTHY

Genesis 15:6.

PAUL

Right. And then, also—Genesis 18:18: "In you all the Gentiles will be blessed."

Timothy finds the second passage and compares them.

TIMOTHY

Okay. What now?

PAUL

(lights a cigarette)

These two passages provide us with the four
words which, when combined correctly, make
my point. Faith. Righteousness. Gentiles and
Blessing.

061. INTERIOR, GALATIA ROOMS—DAY

Apollos is reading Paul's letter aloud to his congregation. As usual, everyone struggles to understand.

APOLLOS

"You foolish Galatians! Just as Abraham
believed God and it was reckoned to him as
righteousness so those who believe are the
descendants of Abraham. And the scripture,
foreseeing that God would justify the
Gentiles by faith alone, declared the gospel
beforehand to Abraham, saying all the
Gentiles shall be blessed in you."

LORI

(jumps up, frustrated)

I can't take it anymore!

LEO

(to Apollos)

So, we don't need to be circumcised?

APOLLOS

Not according to Paul.

LORI

Do you need a graduate school education to
understand this stuff or what! Am I just stupid?

She grabs her bag and heads for the door. An older man, Thomas, follows her.

THOMAS
I'm going back home where we worship bulls!

JASON
(joins them)
Me too! Let's wash ourselves in the blood of
a bull and get on with our lives, alright!

061. INTERIOR, JERUSALEM ROOMS—DAY

Peter kicks over a chair and throws a vase of flowers to the floor. His elderly scribe cringes and shields his head.

PETER
You tell Paul of Tarsus that I, Peter of
Jerusalem, am on my way up there personally
to circumcise the Galatians myself!

062. EXTERIOR, EPHESUS ROOMS—DAY

Paul lays down another letter he has just read. He's concerned. His operation has grown and there are many more scribes and assistants buzzing around him as he thinks. A title card reads: *Ephesus, 56 Common Era.*

PAUL
More trouble in Galatia. We're losing people
to the pagan sacrifice of animals.

TIMOTHY
They're terrified of Peter.

PAUL
Sacrifice. Blood. Animals—people can't
get enough of this stuff.

TIMOTHY
(carefully)
A lot of them would happily be circumcised.

PAUL

Yeah, and a lot of them would happily jump
off a cliff, too, if we said it was okay.

TIMOTHY

And then, of course…
			(lifts another letter)
…there's the Corinthians.

PAUL

			(groans, weary)
What is it this time?

TIMOTHY

			(reads)
"What should we do with meat we have
acquired which was sacrificed to pagan idols?"

PAUL

For crying out loud! We've been through
this a hundred times!

TIMOTHY

We've got to reach some sort of conclusion.

PAUL

Idols don't exist! So, the meat was sacrificed
to nothing and is, therefore, just meat!

Suddenly, Simon runs in, exhausted from having been chased.
Paul waits as he catches his breath.

SIMON

They've got some of our people!

PAUL

Who?

SIMON

The local pagans have dragged Gus and a few
of the others off to the amphitheater!

062. INTERIOR, EPHESUS AMPHITHEATER—DAY

A Greek pagan named Demetrius is giving a speech to a volatile crowd.

> DEMETRIUS
> If Paul and his followers keep gaining in
> popularity around here, turning the people to
> this one true god of theirs, the temple of Artemis
> will be scorned and the goddess herself will be
> deprived of the majesty that brought all Asia
> and the world to worship her here in Ephesus!

The place erupts into hundreds of arguments on all sides. The atmosphere is contentious. Demetrius calls over the uproar—

> DEMETRIUS
> What will happen to our businesses if no one
> comes here to Ephesus and buys our statues
> of the goddess!

And the arguing just escalates. Meanwhile, Paul himself enters and the crowd starts screaming insanely. But—

> PAUL
> We are not temple robbers!

People quiet down and make way for him as he muscles his way to the center.

> CROWD
> Troublemaker! Asshole! You blaspheme the
> goddess!

> PAUL
> I don't say anything about the goddess one way
> or the other! I try to tell people about the Word
> of the Lord!

> DEMETRIUS
> Yeah. Yeah. Yeah. This god who's in each

one of us and who only requires our faith
in his goodness! Big deal!

GEORGE
Paul, face it. It's boring. These people want
ceremony, sacrifice, drama!

PAUL
But our whole religion is nothing but a
ceremonial remembrance of sacrifice—the
one and only sacrifice that matters: God
himself, come down to earth, as a man,
becomes his own son and is sacrificed for
our sins!

This is new for everyone. They quiet down and try to wrap their
minds around it. Even Timothy and Adam pause for thought.
Meanwhile, free associating—

PAUL
Like you people over there wash yourselves
in the blood of the sacrificed bull and believe
you acquire its strength. Just so, our Savior's
blood washes away our sins and saves us
from death.

DEMETRIUS
Are you talking about human sacrifice?

SOMEONE
Sick bastard.

GEORGE
That's obscene!

MAN
Let the guy talk!

WOMAN
(screams)
Cannibals!

People are wrestling and shouting one another down. Paul calls
across to George.

                        PAUL
          You call this boring! These people are ripe for
          a religion with real teeth in it, George.

                     DEMETRIUS
          Pervert! Get outta here! Go back to Cilicia!

Enter the mayor with a contingent of soldiers. He blows a whistle
and the people settle down.

                       MAYOR
          People! People! We are in danger of being
          charged with rioting! Will you all try to
          remember that! The Roman proconsul, maybe
          even the emperor himself, might hear about
          this and, like last time, punish the whole
          population!

The crowd grumbles but disperses. The mayor points to Paul.

                       MAYOR
          Arrest that man.

                        PAUL
          Again? For what?

                       MAYOR
          You cause riots.
                    (comes closer for emphasis)
          Every. Where. You go.

                        PAUL
          I don't cause riots. I say what I have to say.
          The people respond.

                       MAYOR
                    (as he leaves)
          They respond by rioting.

063. EXTERIOR, EPHESUS STREETS—DAY

The crowd follows the soldiers as they drag Paul to jail.

064. INTERIOR, EPHESUS JAIL—DAY

Paul is thrown into a cell. As the door slams shut behind him, he sees another prisoner, Ed, seated on a bench against the wall.

> ED
>
> You're back!

> PAUL
>
> Afraid so.

> ED
>
> So soon?

> PAUL
>
> I'm just popular, I guess.

Just as he sits, there is a commotion at a window above them.

> ADAM
>
> *(off)*
> Paul? Paul, you in there?

> PAUL
>
> *(stands)*
> Adam, yeah, I'm here. What did you learn?

> ADAM
>
> They'll let you out in a few days if we agree
> to leave town right away.

> PAUL
>
> *(to Ed, disappointed)*
> Typical.

> ADAM
>
> What should we do?

PAUL
(paces and thinks)
Organize a meeting. For the night I'm released.
Tell everyone. Find someplace big. And tell the
mayor we'll leave the next morning.

ADAM
Okay.

PAUL
And get me something to write with.

ADAM
Here.

Ed stands and helps catch a number of sheets of loose-leaf that
Adam feeds in through the bars of the open window. A moment
later, some pencils fall in onto the floor.

PAUL
Thanks.

ADAM
Gotta go. See you later.

PAUL
Ed, can I use that bench?

ED
Sure.

Paul kneels on the floor and uses the bench as a desk. Ed looks on
as Paul composes an opening sentence.

PAUL
(writing)
To all God's beloved in Rome, grace to you
and peace from God our Father and the Lord
Jesus Christ…

And he continues to write.

065. INTERIOR, EPHESUS HALL—NIGHT

Timothy arrives and finds hundreds of people gathered there. He locates Adam.

                    ADAM
          Did they release him?

                    TIMOTHY
          He's on his way.

Timothy moves on inside. Adam waits, looking up the street. Paul is approaching, flanked by Gus, Simon, and dozens of others. Those inside crowd into the entrance to welcome him. He comes in, shaking hands, nodding hello, eager to get down to business. He pats Adam on the back reassuringly, then sees Phoebe and hands her his letter.

                    PAUL
          You're Phoebe, right? Here, take this letter
          with you to the church in Rome.

                    ADAM
          But aren't you coming to Rome too?

                    PAUL
          No. It's time I went back to Jerusalem and
          delivered this money I've collected from our
          churches in Macedonia and Achaia.

                    GUS
          It's dangerous for you in Jerusalem.

                    PAUL
          I promised.

                    ADAM
          Let one of us bring it. You can go with Phoebe
          to Rome then continue on to Spain as planned.

Paul moves aside, considering this. He sits and decides:

PAUL

No. I have to make it to Jerusalem first. I have
to enter the Temple one more time.
(sees this troubles them)
Look, there is no way to get to the end except
through the middle. Preaching this gospel to
both the Jews and the Gentiles of Judea is the
very center of the middle.

SIMON

They'll kill you.

PAUL

Probably. But that just means I'm with Jesus
that much faster. Whether I'm alive or dead
I live in Christ. That's the point.

SIMON
(feels faint)
That's hardcore, boss.

Paul pats him on the arm and turns to Gus.

PAUL

Gus, how do we get there?

Gus pulls a map out of his pocket and unfolds it.

GUS

I say overland to Patara where we have some
good people, in buses we rent from Simon's
cousin, then by ship to Antioch where our
trucks are still parked in a bonded lot.

They gather around a table and study the route he's worked out.

066. EXTERIOR, EPHESUS DEPOT—DAY

Hundreds of Paul's people are loading themselves into buses. Gus
checks off lists of names and directs traffic, sending the vehicles
on their way.

067. EXTERIOR, EPHESUS HIGHWAY—DAY

The buses drive off in a long line to Patara.

068. EXTERIOR, JERUSALEM APOSTLE HQ—DAY

Peter looks out at the loud, noisy, turbulent city, frowning. He turns aside and watches as a runner, a young boy, sprints towards him with a letter.

069. EXTERIOR, PATARA DOCK—DAY

Paul and his gang arrive and step down out of the buses at the waterfront. Fellow believers headed by a man named Secundus, greet them. There are also photographers and journalists. Paul is led away discreetly to the back door of a small hotel. Gus, Simon, and Adam approach Secundus.

> SECUNDUS
>
> Glory be to God.

> GUS
>
> Peace be with you.

> SECUNDUS
>
> We received your letter.

> GUS
>
> Good.

> SECUNDUS
>
> Is it true you're on your way to Jerusalem?

> GUS
>
> Yes. We set sail for Antioch in the morning.

> SECUNDUS
>
> I suggest you change plans.

> GUS
>
> What have you heard?

SECUNDUS
Pirates from Cyprus are lying in wait, knowing
Paul is carrying the donations for Jerusalem.
And, besides, the Jews in Antioch have hired
assassins to kill him on arrival.

GUS
What do you suggest?

SECUNDUS
Sail straight across the Mediterranean to
Caesarea.

SIMON
That's a lot more dangerous. Open sea all the
way. And this time of year?

SECUNDUS
Under the circumstances you have little choice.

070. INTERIOR, JERUSALEM APOSTLE HQ—DAY

Peter enters with the letter he's received.

PETER
Paul's on his way.

John grabs the letter. He reads. James comes over and waits.

JAMES
He's bringing the donations, as he said he
would.

PETER
(skeptical)
Apparently.

JOHN
How much?

Peter leans in, points, and shows him the amount.

                              JOHN
  Wow.

071. EXTERIOR, SEA MERCHANT SHIP—DAY

Paul and his people set sail, southeast across the Mediterranean,
towards Caesarea.

072. INTERIOR, JERUSALEM APOSTLE HQ—DAY

Meanwhile—

                              JAMES
            We should make some accommodation for
            him then.

                              PETER
            He's not alone.

                              JAMES
            How many are with him?

073. EXTERIOR, CAESAREA PORT—DAY

Paul and his tribe of a few hundred men, women, and children are
clambering away from the ship and starting to march along the
road to Jerusalem.

074. INTERIOR, JERUSALEM APOSTLE HQ—DAY

                              JAMES
                           (troubled)
            Do you think he knows?

                              PETER
            Knows what?

                              JOHN
            That he's likely to be killed here in Jerusalem.

James looks away. Peter paces, irritated.

PETER

Sure, he knows. I think he almost wants it to
happen.

075. EXTERIOR, JERUSALEM ROAD—DAY

Paul and his people see a truck approaching and make way for it.
The driver stops and leans out.

DRIVER

Is Paul of Tarsus here?

PAUL

That's me.

DRIVER

I have word for you from James in Jerusalem.

He hands a note to Timothy, who takes it, steps aside, and reads it.
He then looks at Paul and hands it to him.

TIMOTHY

They're warning you not to come to Jerusalem.

PAUL

What about the donations?

TIMOTHY

They'll come and meet us out here.

Paul glances at the missive, then hands it to Adam, who looks it
over carefully.

ADAM

He's right. The crowd will kill you.

Paul continues on his way, unconcerned. Timothy looks at the
others. They're worried. Gus comes back over to the driver.

GUS

What's the word in Jerusalem?

DRIVER
The drought's still on. There's been food
shortages. A few riots.
(shifts into gear)
It's tense.

Gus, Simon, Timothy, and Adam turn and look off at Paul way up ahead of them, walking into Jerusalem. They then consider their followers, who are looking to them for guidance. Gus scratches his head and moves on. The crowd follows.

076. INTERIOR, JERUSALEM APOSTLE HQ—DAY

Paul sits amongst the Apostles. In a side room, the accountants are dealing with the donations—piles of cash.

JAMES
Brother, the followers of the Way in and
around Jerusalem have increased tenfold
since we last saw you. They are upright and
peaceful Jews who live by the law and who
accept the teachings of Jesus.
(adjusts tactfully, then)
They are indeed happy, as we are, with your
mission to the Gentiles. But they hear that
you teach the Jews living amongst the
Gentiles now to forsake Moses and the law.

Paul stares at his hands laid flat on the table before him. He composes himself before he speaks.

PAUL
Jesus was the Son of God. He was sent to
live and to die and—by doing so—establish
between God and us a new covenant. This
new covenant abolishes the law. In his death,
we live.

The other Apostles murmur angrily. Most stand up and leave the room, slamming doors. Gradually, it becomes quiet again. Peter restrains himself but speaks forcefully.

                    PETER

You have no authority to claim this. And it
sounds suspiciously like pagan mumbo jumbo.

                    PAUL

I have all the authority I need.

Adam and Timothy sit nearby, hoping for the best but ready for a
brawl. James is calm and steady but losing patience.

                    JAMES

Jesus did not preach the end of the law.

                    PAUL

What Jesus did or did not preach no longer
matters.

Peter stands and knocks over his chair. James rises, hoping to
avoid violence.

                    JAMES

Paul, my friend, go in peace. But we can do
nothing to protect you.

077. EXTERIOR, JERUSALEM—DAY

Paul, Adam, and Timothy come out and join the others waiting
outside.

                    PAUL
                (upbeat)
Okay. That's done.

                    ADAM

What now?

                    PAUL

We have to go to the Temple.

And he starts on his way. But his friends stay put, resistant. Paul
stops and turns back.

                    PAUL
                  (irritated)
            Come on. What?

                  TIMOTHY
            Are you sure you want to do this?

                    PAUL
            It's the whole point. It's why I'm here.

                    GUS
            Please consider the consequences. You're
            more valuable to us alive than dead.

                    PAUL
            From our perspective, maybe. But not from
            God's. Something has to happen here. An
            act. Something all interested parties will
            point to and acknowledge.

He moves on. The others look at each other, troubled and divided. Finally, frustrated, Gus takes charge and does some crisis management:

                    GUS
            Terrence, Malachi: get the women and children
            out of town. Seth, Barnabas, Daniel: lawyers,
            guns, and money.

078. EXTERIOR, JERUSALEM TEMPLE—DAY

The locals see Paul coming and they watch quietly as he enters. They watch as his Gentile associates approach. But Gus and his men stay outside at a safe distance.

079. INTERIOR, JERUSALEM TEMPLE—DAY

Paul's entrance, though meek, is very conspicuous. The Temple is crowded, but people stand aside and make way for him as he crosses the court of the Gentiles and approaches the inner court of the Israelites.

080. EXTERIOR, JERUSALEM TEMPLE—DAY

Outside, his men wait anxiously.

081. INTERIOR, JERUSALEM TEMPLE—DAY

As Paul passes through the barrier and enters the inner court, someone calls to him and the crowd takes notice of this exchange.

                    AMOZ
    Paul!

                    PAUL
             (stops and looks)
    Amoz, the money changer!

                    AMOZ
    Look at this! You could be just any other
    normal citizen visiting Jerusalem during a
    feast!

                    PAUL
    I am all those things.

                    AMOZ
    You're being modest. Your reputation has
    preceded you.

Paul decides it's now or never—

                    PAUL
    I've come to Jerusalem…
             (notices everyone quiets down)
    …to Jerusalem to…
             (feels crowded by strangers)
    …to deliver charitable aid to my friends the
    followers of Jesus.

                    AMOZ
    Your *friends* the followers of Jesus: that's
    a laugh!

                              JESSE
                           (laughing)
              I heard they've put a price on your head.
              Sent out hired assassins!

082. EXTERIOR, JERUSALEM TEMPLE—DAY

                              SIMON
                           (anxious)
              I'm going in.

                               GUS
              Easy! Wait a minute.

                              SIMON
              I can go in as far as the court of the Gentiles,
              right?

                               GUS
              Adam, you go in.

Adam is already up a few steps and peering inside circumspectly.
He comes back to the street, holding his head in his hands.

                              ADAM
              I'm afraid to look.

083. INTERIOR, JERUSALEM TEMPLE—DAY

Paul is setting the record straight for his fellow citizens.

                              PAUL
              Money I collected from the Christian
              communities in Macedonia and—

                              AMOZ
              We've heard rumors of riots in Ephesus,
              armed conflict in Antioch.

Now everybody—hundreds of people—move in closer to hear
Paul's reply. He considers the situation, looking across at the

barrier separating the outer court from the inner. As usual, opposition only makes him more forceful and eloquent.

PAUL
Of course, there is conflict and riot, discord and mayhem. What do you expect? The righteousness of an angry god is about to be visited upon a hopelessly corrupt world!

Silence. No one is impressed. They wait for more.

PAUL
And I, Paul, the Apostle of Christ, I am the instrument!

Now there is threatening movement and grumbling. Undaunted—

PAUL
(continues)
There is no more Jew! There is no more Gentile! No more man, no more woman, no more Egyptian, no more Persian. In Christ Jesus we are all one!

YOUNG MAN
Damn! Righteous, brother! Word up!

Everyone looks at this young man and he realizes he should just shut up. He does. But Paul is encouraged.

PAUL
This temple might still be standing. This barrier here between the court of the Gentiles and the court of the Israelites might still exist. But it is meaningless.

Paul looks around himself at the bustling multitude and points to the *Devir*, the holy of holies, the off-limits center of the Temple.

PAUL
You can't keep God in a box!

                    JESSE
Shut him up!

                   WOMAN
Sacrilege!

                    PAUL
The Torah is a thing of the past, words in a
book. The community of the faithful waiting
for Jesus is a house where God lives!

Dead silence. Paul sweats, gulps, and waits. The crowd watches
him, deeply suspicious and threatened. Then Simon is there all of
a sudden, on the far side of the barrier in the court of the Gentiles.
He holds out his hand and calls quietly across to Paul.

                   SIMON
Boss, come on, let's get outta here.

Paul looks over. Simon waits. Then—

                    PAUL
Yes, my friend, God is no longer in this
house.

Stillness. Then—pandemonium. The crowd swells like an ocean
and descends upon Paul.

084. EXTERIOR, JERUSALEM TEMPLE—DAY

Paul's friends are trying to see and hear from out on the crowded
steps.

                   ADAM
What's happening?

                  CITIZEN 1
They've got him.

                  TIMOTHY
What did he do?

CITIZEN 2

He brought one of his Gentile friends into the
inner court!

TIMOTHY

No, he didn't!

CITIZEN 2

How do you know?

ADAM

Because we're his Gentile friends and we're
standing right here!

GUS
(notices)
Hey, where's Simon?

And the riot inside starts spilling out onto the street.

085. INTERIOR, JERUSALEM TEMPLE—DAY

Paul is being pummeled by hundreds of different fists and tossed
about over the heads of the crowd, swinging hard at all comers.

086. EXTERIOR, JERUSALEM TEMPLE—DAY

The whole neighborhood is a war zone now.

087. INTERIOR, JERUSALEM FORTRESS—DAY

Paul is dragged in by Roman soldiers, delirious with pain. The
tribune, Claudius, is a very busy man. He looks up from his
paperwork, distracted.

CLAUDIUS

Are you the Egyptian maniac?

PAUL
(coughs up blood)
I think there's been a mistake.

CLAUDIUS
(drops his pen and stands)
You are the leader of the terrorists who move
about the crowds at festival time stabbing
people indiscriminately!

PAUL
I am a Jew, from Tarsus in Cilicia.

CLAUDIUS
Oh, forgive me.
(sits back down)
The situation is tense here in Jerusalem, as
always—but more so than usual.

PAUL
I've been away from the city for some time.

CLAUDIUS
(writing)
Good for you. Some Jewish fanatic
assassinated the high priest of the Temple a
few months ago and the mob has been restless
ever sense.
(pushes aside his work)
Now, look, we don't like riots. What happened
over there at the Temple?

PAUL
I was accused of bringing a Gentile inside.

CLAUDIUS
Now, why would you do that?

PAUL
I didn't.

CLAUDIUS
Then, why would they accuse you?

Paul finds a handkerchief and wipes his face.

PAUL

Because I preach the gospel of Jesus.

CLAUDIUS

Jesus?

PAUL

Yes.

CLAUDIUS

So, you're one of them.

PAUL

Well, sir, if I can make a distinction—

CLAUDIUS

No. You may not.
(stands)
You Jesus Followers are my biggest problem
recently.
(to the soldiers)
Take him away and flog him till he admits
what he did.

They start to do this, but—

PAUL

Is it legal to flog a Roman citizen?

The soldiers stop and look back at Claudius. The Roman functionary is intrigued. He comes out from behind his desk and approaches Paul.

CLAUDIUS

You're a Roman citizen?

PAUL

Yes.

CLAUDIUS

It cost me a large sum of money to purchase

my citizenship.
> *(considers Paul's attire)*
You don't appear to be a very wealthy man.

                         PAUL
I was *born* a citizen.

                       CLAUDIUS
> *(genuinely impressed)*
Okay. Okay. Pardon me. We'll look into this.
In the meantime, you'll remain in custody.

                         PAUL
Thank you.

                       CLAUDIUS
As well you should.
> *(at window)*
That mob out there wants to tear you to pieces.

088. INTERIOR, JERUSALEM FORTRESS CELL—DAY

Paul is thrown into the cell. As the door closes behind him he just
stands there and gazes at the floor, another epileptic fit coming on.
He falls to the floor and begins shaking violently.

089. INTERIOR, PARIS BASTILLE—DAY

Paul wakes, lifts his head and pulls himself up off the floor. He
sees he is sharing the cell with another man about his own age but
dressed in the manner of the 18th century in Europe.

                         PAUL
Where am I?

                         PAINE
The Bastille. Paris, France. 1793.

                         PAUL
> *(dusts himself off)*
Shit.

He comes over and offers the stranger his hand.

                    PAUL
          Paul of Tarsus, Apostle to the Gentiles.

                    PAINE
          Paine. Thomas Paine. Author, inventor,
          missionary of world revolution. Here,
          sit down.

He makes room for Paul on the bench. A riot can be heard outside
in the streets.

                    PAUL
          What's going on out there?

                    PAINE
          The revolution.

                    PAUL
          Against Rome?

                    PAINE
          Rome fell over fifteen hundred years ago.

                    PAUL
                 (startled)
          No!

                    PAINE
          It's true.

                    PAUL
          It must have been the Messiah! The Second
          Coming!

                    PAINE
          No, barbarians from the North. Germans, Swedes,
          Belgians. They worshipped trees.

Paul is demoralized all over again.

PAUL

What year you say it was?

PAINE

1793.

PAUL

And Jesus has still not returned?

PAINE

No. But his absence, and the threat that he
will return, have been like a boot on the throat
of mankind ever since.
(stands and paces)
Religion, you see, is a human invention set up
to terrify and enslave mankind and monopolize
power and profit.

PAUL

Sit back down, my friend. You're raving like
a lunatic.

PAINE
(sits again)
Reason is my god. Reason.

Now Paul goes to the window and looks out, puzzled, at the riot in
the street.

PAUL

So, who are they?

PAINE

The French.

PAUL

What are they revolting against?

PAINE

Everything. The world order. Including the
church.

PAUL

What church?

PAINE

Ultimately, you were hugely effective. Your
successors converted all the Gentiles and
formed something called the Catholic Church.
They rearranged the books of the Jewish
covenant and added a new one, The New
Testament, largely based on these letters
you've been writing. Now, calling
themselves Christians, they generally
persecute Jews and blame them for all sorts
of mysterious problems with the weather
and the economy. It'll get worse before it gets
better, I think.

Paul is dumbstruck. Trembling, he sits back down.

PAUL

My God, what have I done!

Paine goes back to the window and watches the street.

PAINE

But now, just a few years after the glorious
revolution, taken up in the name of liberty,
equality, and fraternity—now, in a thorough
repudiation of all inherited political and
social prejudice, my fellow revolutionaries
have thrown the baby out with the bath water.
They've become barbarians without any
morality at all.
    (points)
Look, there, a priest is being tortured.

PAUL

Has God forsaken me? Has he brought me
here to crush my soul? Have I been shown
these things as a punishment for my pride,
my arrogance?

PAINE

I doubt it. There is a first cause of some kind,
call it god if you like, that generated the
universe perhaps. But it does not interfere
with the world. That would be what is called
a miracle. And there are no miracles.

PAUL
(throws his arms wide)
What do you call this!?

PAINE
(looks around)
What do I call this? A bad dream. The dark
night of the soul. Hell. The world as we know
it is not going away as you so fervently hope,
my friend. It is what it is. And if it can be
changed for the better, we ourselves are going
to have to do it ourselves.

090. INTERIOR, JERUSALEM FORTRESS—DAY

Anthony, the soldier who joined Paul and Timothy in Philippi, is
asking directions of other Roman soldiers.

091. INTERIOR, JERUSALEM FORTRESS—DAY

Anthony is before Claudius.

CLAUDIUS
And what do you consider the situation to be?

ANTHONY
Difficult. Word is there's a band of fanatics
from Antioch who have pledged themselves to
killing Paul or starving themselves trying.

CLAUDIUS
(calculates)
How many of his friends are there? How many
came with him to Jerusalem?

ANTHONY

A few hundred.

CLAUDIUS

Can you control them?

ANTHONY

I can get them out of town.

CLAUDIUS

Good. Do so.

ANTHONY

But what about Paul?

CLAUDIUS

He has not committed a crime against Rome.
He is accused of an offence against Jewish
law. And, of course, long-suffering Rome is
obliged to provide them with the opportunity
to prosecute. But I don't want to give them
that opportunity when there are hundreds of
his followers in town.

ANTHONY

Maybe we should get Paul out of town instead.

CLAUDIUS

Sooner or later, of course. Since he's from
Cilicia, the Governor of Judea at Caesarea
will have jurisdiction in any event.

ANTHONY

It would be quicker and easier than dispersing
his followers.

CLAUDIUS
(grateful, relieved)
Yes. Right. Good. It's not really my problem,
is it? Requisition a truck and I'll assign you
some soldiers.

092. INTERIOR, JERUSALEM FORTRESS—NIGHT

Soldiers come and drag Paul out of his cell.

093. EXTERIOR, JERUSALEM FORTRESS—NIGHT

Anthony watches from up front in the truck's cab, looking on as Paul is brought out into the courtyard and thrown into the back of the truck. The doors are slammed, the soldiers climb in, and the truck drives off.

094. INTERIOR, CAESAREA FORTRESS—DAY

The procurator, Felix, lowers the papers containing the charges against Paul.

                              FELIX
                 You're a Roman citizen?

                              PAUL
          Yeah.

                              FELIX
                 To what province do you belong?

                              PAUL
          Cilicia.

There are many other prisoners waiting in line. Felix hands off the paperwork and gestures for the next prisoner.

                              FELIX
                 I will give you a hearing when your accusers
                 arrive. Next.
                         (then, to his assistant)
          Cilicia?

                              ASSISTANT
          In Syria.

Paul is led away.

FELIX

Can't we get in touch with the governor of
Syria and see if we can dump this maniac off
on them?

ASSISTANT

I doubt it.

FELIX
(to next prisoner)
And you, what's your name?

095. INTERIOR, CAESAREA FORTRESS—DAY

A week later, the high priest of the Sanhedrin in Jerusalem,
Parmenas and a functionary called an accuser, make their case
before Felix.

ACCUSER

This man is an agitator amongst all the Jews
of the world. The ringleader of a sect!

Felix looks from the accuser to Paul, who can hardly be bothered.

PAUL

I admit to you, that according to the Way,
which they call a sect, I worship the God
of our ancestors, believing everything laid
down according to the law or written in
the prophets.

FELIX

Yes, I know a good deal about the Way. You
insist that the Jewish Messiah has come and
gone already. I find that quite novel.

PARMENAS

It's heresy!

FELIX

No, faith in a Messiah—some warrior king

come to lead a revolt against the good
management of Roman law is more than just
heresy. It's a punishable offense. That Paul
and his crowd believe a misguided young
rabbi crucified twenty years ago was this
Messiah—well, that's more than a bit
comforting for my superiors back in Rome.

PARMENAS
We insist the prisoner be brought back to
Jerusalem and stand trial there!

Already leaving, Felix stops and turns back to them all. He looks
from Parmenas to Paul.

FELIX
Paul?

PAUL
I appeal unto Caesar.

ACCUSER
(throws down his paperwork)
Son of a bitch!

PAUL
Hey! Neither against the law of the Jews, nor
against the Temple, nor against Caesar have
I offended at all!

FELIX
Gentlemen, I'm sorry. He's a Roman citizen.
He's allowed to do this.

PARMENAS
(to Paul)
What do you mean: you have not offended!
You violate the law at every turn!

FELIX
Take the prisoner away.

The hearing breaks up amongst curses and shouting. Felix walks down a hallway, turns into another, descends some stairs, and finds himself in a small courtyard where Paul is being led back to his cell by Anthony. Paul and his escort stop.

                    FELIX
          I'm sending you to Rome.

                    PAUL
          As you wish.

                    FELIX
          You could have been set free if you had not
          appealed unto Caesar. It could've ended here.
          I have the jurisdiction.

                    PAUL
          I have to let Caesar know the Gospel. It's
          important.

                    FELIX
          You're likely to be executed in Rome.

                    PAUL
          I'll risk it.

                    FELIX
              (walks on, unconcerned)
          Good luck.

Paul and Anthony move on. Paul is already making plans.

                    PAUL
          We've got some serious damage control to do,
          my friend.

096. EXTERIOR, SHIP AT SEA—DAY

Paul is back by the stern, handcuffed, but smoking and talking with Luke as Anthony approaches. The sea is rough and the sky is darkening.

PAUL

And in the Antonia Fortress I was given this
further revelation from the Lord our God,
brought to a place called France during some
revolution or other.
(sees Anthony)
Anthony, Luke. Luke, Anthony. Luke's a
writer from Syracuse.

ANTHONY

How do you do.

PAUL
(continues his story)
So, anyway… it's imperative that the Gospel
not be misconstrued and institutionalized.
This was the meaning of the vision I received.
I've got to warn Caesar to spot the emergence
of this sinister church that will reshape the
gospel into a dogma so repellent that Jesus,
the Messiah, won't ever return.
(smokes, looks out at the sea)
Where on earth does our illustrious captain
think he's headed now?

ANTHONY

He wants to pass by Crete and head on to Italy.

PAUL

He's nuts. It's too late in the year. The
weather's turning.

ANTHONY

The ship's owner is on board too. He wants
to make one more profitable delivery of grain
to Rome before the season ends.

097. EXTERIOR, SHIP AT SEA PILOT DECK—DAY

Later, the ship's owner and the captain are trying to get rid of
Paul.

CAPTAIN
(to Anthony of Paul)
Can't you control him?

OWNER
(to captain)
Who is he?

CAPTAIN
He's a prisoner.

ANTHONY
He's very widely traveled, though, and a
prosperous businessman.

PAUL
And I know what it's like to be in a shipwreck.

CAPTAIN
(worried)
Hey! Keep it down.

OWNER
Then why are you a prisoner being taken to
Rome?

PAUL
That's got nothing to do with it.
(then, to the captain)
Listen, sail under the lee of Crete, dock, and
stay put till spring.

OWNER
I can't afford to do that.

PAUL
(disregards owner)
Look, Captain, you know as well as me this
time of year you're likely to get pummeled
by a northeaster and driven before the storm
all the way to who knows where!

CAPTAIN
Soldier, cuff him and get him down below!

PAUL
You'll wish you had listened to me!

The owner watches Paul go and then returns to the captain.

OWNER
You know, in the old days we would have
just thrown him overboard.

CAPTAIN
Please! Sir! Enough.

098. EXTERIOR, SHIP AT SEA—DAY

Paul and Anthony climb down to a lower deck and rejoin Luke, who is looking out at the threatening weather.

LUKE
Not long now.

099. EXTERIOR, SHIP AT SEA—NIGHT

A violent storm. The ship is tossed around like a cork on the sea.

100. EXTERIOR, SHIP AT SEA—DAY

The storm has lessened and there is light in the sky. But the fog is dense. Luke is sick as a dog and leans on the railing watching Anthony talk with the captain and the owner.

CAPTAIN
We've got to lighten the ship.

OWNER
And throw the prisoners overboard.

ANTHONY
No.

OWNER

We have twenty-five prisoners on board. That's
weight. And besides we've got to feed them.

ANTHONY

It's my responsibility to bring those prisoners
to Rome.

CAPTAIN

We've been driven before the storm for
fourteen days. We're hundreds of miles off
course. Provisions are running low.

SAILOR
(approaches)
Captain, we've taken more soundings. Fifteen
fathoms. Five less than yesterday.

The captain looks at Anthony.

ANTHONY
(resolute)
Don't harm the prisoners and don't toss the
provisions overboard. We may need them
wherever it is we wash up.

And at that moment: BANG!!!! The ship hits rocks and lists dan-
gerously. Paul wakes from a nap.

PAUL
(refreshed)
What's happening?

LUKE

We've run aground!

ANTHONY

Come on! Starboard!

Everyone runs for cover. The ship cracks, tilts, and shivers. The
captain struggles to his feet.

CAPTAIN

Lower the boats!

OWNER

Save the cargo!

101. EXTERIOR, BENEATH THE SEA—DAY

The ship having sunk, Paul, his friends, and the others are drifting down into the depths.

102. EXTERIOR, MALTA SHORE—DAY

Some longshoremen are standing on the docks watching Paul, Anthony, Luke, and a few other survivors drift towards them on debris from the ship. A title card announces: *Malta.*

103. INTERIOR, UNION HALL—NIGHT

The Maltese longshoremen are throwing a party for the survivors. Their shop steward is a man named Lenny and he's talking with Anthony.

LENNY

There won't be any ships coming this way
until spring. You'll have to sit out the winter.

ANTHONY

Can you afford to keep us all that long?

LENNY

A lot of the cargo washed ashore too. We'll
call that the price of room and board. How
many of these guys are prisoners?

ANTHONY
(looks around)
Most of them.

LENNY

You'll take responsibility?

ANTHONY
Have you got work for them to do?

LENNY
Sure. Who are those two intellectuals over
there?

Anthony sees he is referring to Paul and Luke who are deep in
conversation with a few longshoremen and prisoners.

PAUL
For ages us Jews have eaten the body of the
ritually sacrificed lamb. But we did not drink
its blood because God had commanded us
not to eat meat with life still in it. That is to
say, blood.

SEAMAN
(shyly)
That's pretty sensible.

LONGSHOREMAN
(encouraged)
Yeah, it's a sensible God you've got.

PAUL
Instead, in Egypt, we splashed the blood on
the lintels of our houses as a sign to the angel
of death to pass over that home.

SEAMAN
This God of yours has an angel of death?

PAUL
He destroyed the Egyptians.

PRISONER
And Jesus was this God?

PAUL
Made man.

LUKE
But he was crucified and died.

PAUL
(clarifies)
As a sacrifice.

They're all working hard to follow.

PRISONER
(ventures)
Like… Like the Passover lamb?

PAUL
Exactly! Luke, you got something to write
with?

Luke scrambles for his notebook and pen while Paul hurries on, following this train of associations.

PAUL
Jesus was the lamb and his death saves us in
a new way. Whenever we come together in
memory of his death, we drink his blood
exactly because it has life in it.

PRISONER
For real?

PAUL
No! This was Jesus' genius. This is why I
know he was God. He took a piece of bread
and called it his body. Then he took a glass
of wine and called it his blood…

Meanwhile, back across the room—

LENNY
That older guy commands an awful lot of
attention from this riffraff. He ain't some
kind of agitator, is he?

ANTHONY
(evades)
He's a maker of tents.

LENNY
(delighted)
Is he? Great! He'll be useful this winter. Got
lots of repairs to be done. Sailcloth and so on.

104. EXTERIOR, MALTA DOCKS—DAY

It's late winter and snow is falling. Paul is mending sailcloth by
himself out at the end of the pier. Luke approaches.

LUKE
Have you heard? There's a ship from
Alexandria supposed to stop here in a week
or two.

PAUL
Is it spring already?

LUKE
Nearly.
(sits, then)
Do you think you'll be acquitted in Rome?

PAUL
Maybe. The important thing is to warn Caesar
to keep a look out for this emerging church.
If he doesn't chop my head off, I'll try and
collect some money from my friends and
continue on to Spain.

LUKE
Spain?

PAUL
No one has preached the Gospel in Spain yet.

Luke is amused at the man's energy.

                    LUKE
Why go to the far-flung reaches of the
empire? Make your point in the capital and
the rest of the world will follow.

                    PAUL
The Gospel is alive and well in all those
places. God wants me in the provinces. What
about you?

                    LUKE
I'm not going all the way to Rome just yet.
The ship will stop at Syracuse. I'll go home
for a while.

                    PAUL
And write your masterpiece?

                    LUKE
Yeah. Maybe. I hope so. I think it's time I try.

                    PAUL
What will you write about?

                    LUKE
Maybe I'll write about you.

                    PAUL
Don't waste your ink. Jesus Christ is what you
ought to be writing about.

                    LUKE
              (shrugs)
All I know about Jesus Christ is what I've
learned from you.

                    PAUL
          (nods, satisfied)
Well, I guess, that's something.

They fall silent and watch the snow falling on the waves.

105. INTERIOR, ROME JAIL—DAY

Luke is with the desk sergeant and waits as the man flips through some paperwork.

                              LUKE
                           (explains)
                    That was the last time I saw him. When I got
                    off the ship at Syracuse.

The sergeant is having trouble making sense of the paperwork.

                            SERGEANT
                    Paul? Of Tarsus? I think so. Hold on.
                           (calls down the hall)
                    Hey! Armando! We got a guy named Paul
                    downstairs?

                            ARMANDO
                             (off)
                    Paul?

                            SERGEANT
                    From Tarsus!

Armando enters.

                            ARMANDO
                    The Cilician crackpot?

                            SERGEANT
                    Whatever. This paperwork is for shit, Armando.

                            ARMANDO
                    You mean the big mouth?

                            SERGEANT
                    Tough guy.

                            ARMANDO
                    A Jew, right—one of those Christian types?

They look at Luke.

LUKE

Yeah.

ARMANDO

He was here a few weeks ago. Been here for
a year, at least. But you know since the fire…

Armando just shrugs.

SERGEANT
(elaborates)
Since the emperor pegged the fire on these
Christian Jews, they've been dropping like
flies.

Luke looks aside and pictures it in his head—

106. EXTERIOR, ROME COURTYARD—DAY

The executioner stands waiting with his bloodied sword. Bodies
are being dragged away. Paul steps up with his hands tied behind
his back. He's allowed one last puff on his cigarette. Then:
SWOOSH!!!! His head is cut off.

107. INTERIOR, PHOEBE'S APARTMENT—DAY

Phoebe is busy packing a suitcase. Luke rushes in, throws the bolt
on the door, and steps closer.

PHOEBE

I've got to get out of town. The neighbors
told the cops I'm a Christian.

LUKE

Give me the letters.

PHOEBE
(hands him the shoebox)
What did you learn at the prison?

                              LUKE
        Not much. He was locked up for over a year.
        After that, no one knows. He was either acquitted
        or had his head chopped off a few days ago.

                             PHOEBE
                         (sits, worried)
        If he had been acquitted, he would have come
        to see us.

                              LUKE
        Maybe he thought he'd be putting you and
        your friends in danger if he did.

                             PHOEBE
        Maybe.

A young man, Jude, appears outside on the fire escape. He throws
open the window.

                              JUDE
        You ready?

                             PHOEBE
        Yeah.

                              JUDE
        Let's go. Quick.

Phoebe grabs her things and climbs out onto the fire escape. She
turns back to Luke.

                             PHOEBE
        Take care of those letters, Luke.

Luke nods. Phoebe and Jude scurry down the fire escape. Luke
hears them drive away. He sits there a moment and then has an
idea, tilts his head, and speaks to himself out loud:

                              LUKE
        But, then, on the other hand—maybe.

A title card announces: *Spain.*

108. EXTERIOR, SPAIN RESTAURANT—DAY

Several Japanese tourists thrill to the charms of a pretty, virtuoso flamenco dancer as Paul holds forth at a nearby table.

> PAUL
> God is good and merciful.

> ALFONSO
> *(struggling)*
> Even to our enemies?

> PAUL
> This whole enemy thing is an illusion. As far as God is concerned, we're all just a bunch of losers. No matter where we come from.

> ALFONSO
> But you say he loves us.

> PAUL
> Yeah.

> ALFONSO
> So, he loves us because we are losers?

> PAUL
> *(sighs)*
> Lord, give me strength to continue!

The lady of the house comes by with a new pitcher.

> ISABELLA
> *Señor* Paul, have some more wine! Alfonso, don't upset him so much!

She pours. But Paul stands when he sees his current assistant approaching: a fat, lazy, younger man infatuated with the pretty dancer.

PAUL

No, my friends, I must be on my way! Sancho!
Saddle our steed!

ISABELLA

No, *señor*!

Sancho drinks the last of Paul's glass and collapses at the table.

SANCHO

I don't know why your worship wants to
start on this frightful adventure! It'll be the
end of us!

Paul lifts a tall staff he needs to walk with, kicks Sancho in the
ass, then grabs him by the arm and leads the way to a busted-up
motorcycle with a sidecar. Sancho climbs awkwardly into the
sidecar as Paul mounts the bike, holding his staff. Everyone
comes to see them off. Even the flamenco dancer stops her
performance and comes to wave goodbye. Paul kick-starts the
machine and it coughs into action. He pats the gas tank like a
horse's neck and looks up at the sky.

PAUL

Observe, loyal and faithful squire, the darkness of this night, its strange silence!

SANCHO

Sir, the sun is still high and the people are
singing!

Paul lowers his goggles, dons his helmet, slips into gear, and
prepares to depart.

PAUL

No, my friend, believe me: the night is far
gone and the day is at hand!

They ride away with everyone dancing after them.

The End ~

The Book of Life

01. EXTERIOR, AIRPORT—DAY

James is a homeless man outside the arrivals gate studying the sky over New York with an old pair of binoculars—

> JAMES
> *(recites)*
> "See, I am sending my messenger ahead
> of you, who will prepare your way; the
> voice of one crying out in the wilderness."

A jet cuts across the sky and lands on the runway and James kneels, studying the travelers passing by him, addressing each one in turn as if he or she were the Messiah.

> JAMES
> Forgive me, Jesus, for I have sinned!
> Have mercy on us now and at the hour
> of our death!

A businessman stops, flags down a taxi, and tosses James a coin. A woman pauses nearby and looks around for the bus stop. James reaches out to her.

> JAMES
> Forgive me, Jesus, for I have sinned!
> Have mercy on us now and at the hour
> of our death!

She falls back and moves away, frightened.

02. INTERIOR, AIRPORT—DAY

Jesus Christ and his personal assistant, Magdalena, stride purposefully through the crowd, looking for the exit. He is a handsome man in a well-tailored business suit and she is an alert and attractive young woman.

03. EXTERIOR, AIRPORT—DAY

They step outside and James grabs the hem of Jesus' jacket.

JAMES

Forgive me, Jesus, for I have sinned! Have
mercy on us now and at the hour of our death!

Jesus stops and regards him with disinterested attention. He
touches James' brow and moves off towards a taxi. Magdalena,
seeing James is surprised, reassures him:

MAGDALENA

Relax.

She follows Jesus to a waiting taxi while James looks on, curious.

JESUS

(voiceover)

I could never get used to that part of the job;
the power and the glory; the threat of divine
vengeance. Mercy…

04. EXTERIOR, HIGHWAY—DAY

The taxi drives through the Midtown Tunnel, approaching New
York City. And Jesus continues to muse:

JESUS

(voiceover)

But I persevered. I was about my father's
business. And I was the good son. It was the
morning of December thirty-first, 1999,
when I returned, at last, to judge the living
and the dead. Though still—and perhaps
always—I had my doubts.

05. EXTERIOR, NEW YORK CITY STREETS—DAY

A likable but untrustworthy gambler named Dave, in a jacket way
too light for the season, is hurrying along when he sees something
in the sky and stops. Something like a huge shadow passes
quickly over the city and Dave blinks to make sure he is not
seeing things. But whatever it was has now disappeared and Dave,
unconcerned, moves to a newsstand. Tossing some coins to the

newsagent, he grabs a paper and scans the headlines: *Last Day of the Century—Believers Pray for The End!* This means nothing to Dave and he pages through to the sports section before remembering to buy a lottery ticket. Taking the ticket, he folds his paper and steps away. Still glancing up at the sky, he nearly gets run down by a taxi and jumps back to the sidewalk, startled. He notices some stressed-out, deeply preoccupied professional, Satan, standing in a doorway watching all this. Satan shrugs and walks away. Dave does too, only mildly embarrassed.

06. INTERIOR, HOTEL LOBBY—DAY

Jesus and Magdalena enter the chic hotel and approach the front desk. The busy desk clerk attends to them.

                         CLERK
        Checking in?

                         JESUS
        We have a reservation.

Magdalena's mobile phone rings. She studies the incoming number and glances at her boss.

                       MAGDALENA
                     (apprehensive)
        Rome.

Jesus shakes his head, refusing the call, and Magdalena steps aside to deal with it herself:

                       MAGDALENA
                     (into phone)
        Hello. Yes. No. Impossible. Sorry.

                         CLERK
        What name is the reservation under, sir?

                         JESUS
                  (looks around, lies)
        Mister and Missus D.W. Griffith.

CLERK

And how many nights will you be staying,
Mister Griffith?

JESUS

Just one.

Magdalena returns from across the lobby, cutting short the phone
call with Rome—

MAGDALENA

Look, I'm sorry. You have the wrong number.

And she hangs up. She and Jesus start for the elevator, but stop,
seeing Satan watching them from the top of the stairs at the mezzanine level. The archfiend smirks sadly and glances away. They
are not surprised to see him, but Magdalena wants to go up and
give him a piece of her mind. Jesus grabs her arm and leads her
away instead.

07. INTERIOR, HOTEL ROOM—DAY

A seasoned bodyguard, Magdalena checks out the suite as Jesus
strolls in and looks out at the city.

JESUS
(voiceover)
I feared my father's wrath. His love was a
burden. He knew this about me too; my
ambivalence. But we shared the blame, he
and I. He made me a man as well as a god
and I? I felt myself, well, blessed.

As Magdalena finishes casing the joint, he finds the minibar, gets
himself a drink, and sits.

JESUS
(wistful)
This is the hour of trial, Magdalena. The good
and the bad, together, they question themselves.
And me? Yes, me. I wonder.

He stands again and looks down into the streets.

                    JESUS
              (continues)
     I like this city.
              (then, resigned)
     Call the lawyers.

08. INTERIOR, HOTEL LOBBY BAR—DAY

Dave enters and walks through the lobby trying to appear better dressed than he is. Approaching the lobby bar, he pauses, surprised to see the troubled man he saw earlier—Satan—seated at the bar with a whiskey. The waitress, Edie, appears to be Dave's girlfriend. They kiss affectionately.

                    DAVE
     Good morning, Edie. I'll have a coffee.

                    EDIE
     Will you be able to pay for it?

                    DAVE
     What? You mean, right away?

                    EDIE
     Soon.

                    DAVE
     It's a distinct possibility. I feel lucky today.
     I've got twenty dollars which I, in fact,
     borrowed from a friend, riding on a vastly
     underrated long shot in the first race of the
     day.
              (glances at Satan)
     Cheer up, mack. Tomorrow is a new century.
     Where's your holiday spirit?

                    SATAN
              (despondent)
     It's all over.

DAVE

No. It's just the beginning. Pull yourself
together. Here, take the sports section.

SATAN

You saw it, didn't you?

DAVE

Saw what?

SATAN

In the sky. You know… You saw it too.

Glad there was, in fact, something he saw, Dave sets aside his
paper and comes closer to Satan.

DAVE

You saw that?

SATAN

It's all over.

DAVE

What the hell was it?

SATAN

A sign.

DAVE

Of what?

SATAN

The end. The end of existence, reality, history,
whatever you want to call it. It's finished,
over, done. God's tolerance for you stupid
human beings has reached its end.

Dave pats him on the back and leaves him alone.

DAVE

Edie, get my unbalanced friend here a cup of

coffee, will ya.

EDIE

Will he be able to pay for it?

DAVE

(to Satan)

Hey, chuckles, you got any money?

Satan drags out his wallet and distractedly lays hundreds of dollars on the bar. Edie approaches with the coffee, but he gestures for her to forget it. Instead, he nudges his empty whiskey glass forward and intones:

SATAN

"Rejoice then, you heavens and those of you
who dwell in them! But woe to the earth and
the sea, for the devil has come down to you
with great wrath because he knows that his
time is short!"

(adds as Edie pours)

Revelation, 12:12.

(sips, then)

Not, of course, my favorite passage.

Edie comes back down the bar to Dave.

EDIE

Many people believe the world is going to
end tonight.

DAVE

You don't believe that, do you?

EDIE

There is a preacher on the radio and that's
all he ever talks about. He says that the
planets and the stars are all lined up the
right way now and that the prophecies have
been fulfilled. He says that when Jesus
returns to earth, he is going to gather

around him 144,000 good souls and then
destroy everyone else.

                    DAVE
Why do you *listen* to that crap?

Edie is not sure. She shrugs and turns away.

                    EDIE
I like the hymns.

09. INTERIOR, LAW OFFICE RECEPTION—DAY

The quick-witted, highly competent receptionist deals with the
filing as she handles the overloaded telephone switchboard:

                RECEPTIONIST
Armageddon Armageddon and Jehoshaphat.
How may I direct your call? Thank you.
Armageddon Armageddon and Jehoshaphat.
How may I direct your call? Thank you.
Armageddon Armageddon and Jehoshaphat.
How may I direct your call? He's not in right
now. Can you call back later? I doubt it.

A bike messenger arrives with a parcel. She drops the filing and
aims a handgun at his chest.

                RECEPTIONIST
Excuse me, can I help you? Hands out of your
pockets!
        (checks parcel's addressee, then)
Thanks. Okay. Leave it there. Scram.

The messenger leaves the package on the desk, backs away, and
flees.

                RECEPTIONIST
        (answers next call)
Armageddon Armageddon and Jehoshaphat.
How may I direct your call? Please hold.

She changes lines and and waits for her boss to pick up.

                    LAWYER
          (off)
    Yeah?

                    RECEPTIONIST
    Excuse me, sir, the call you're waiting for
    is on line two.

10. INTERIOR, LAW OFFICE—DAY

The harried, impatient lawyer grabs the phone and barks into it.

                    LAWYER
    Where the hell have you been! This is no
    time to hesitate! We've got trouble, big
    trouble! The adversary won't settle for
    arbitration. He thinks he can take this to
    the regular courts and win! Of course, he's
    bluffing! But we're in no position to tempt
    fate! Look, you know what your father wants!
    Quit stalling!

11. INTERIOR, HOTEL ROOM—DAY

Jesus hangs up, puts the phone aside, and scratches his head.

                    JESUS
    I remember the Flood, Babel, Sodom and
    Gomorrah. It was before your time, Magdalena.
    My father, he is an angry God. To him, the
    law is everything. Still, today, attorneys
    are his favorites.
          (stands to go)
    Come on. Let's get on with it.

12. INTERIOR, HOTEL BAR & LOBBY—DAY

Business is slow and Edie is listening to a radio evangelist while
Satan tries to read the newspaper at a table near the entrance. The

broadcast makes him increasingly agitated.

EVANGELIST
(on radio)

It'll be ugly, the end of the world. Carnage like
you've never seen before. An unimaginably
immense cosmic catastrophe out of which,
though, will arise a new world, which will be
nothing less than a new Eden. Because of our
neglect for the Lord we must be punished by
famine and pestilence, war and captivity, we
must be subjected to a judgment so severe that it
will make a clean break with our guilty past. The
day of wrath has come when the sun and the
moon and the stars will be darkened, when the
heavens are rolled up together and the earth
shaken. The day has come when the unbelievers
are to be cast down and utterly destroyed. But
the righteous living, together with the righteous
dead, now resurrected, will be assembled before
God and he will dwell there amongst them
as their ruler and judge!

Satan sighs irritably, closes his paper, and looks down at the front
desk, where Jesus hands over his room key to the desk clerk and
receives, in exchange, another very special key the clerk takes
ceremoniously from a safety deposit box. Satan comes forward
and leans out over the railing of the mezzanine level, anxious, but
keeping his distance. Magdalena silently dares him to interfere.
He doesn't. Jesus and Magdalena leave the hotel just as Dave
comes running in off the street, clearly pursued by someone. Once
safe inside, he composes himself and heads for the bar. He climbs
the stairs to the mezzanine three steps at a time, glancing furtively
back at the entrance. Arriving, he falls into a chair. Satan joins
him.

SATAN

What, you lose?

DAVE

Hey! It was a long shot. Gimme a break.

                    SATAN
          Do you really want to win?

                    DAVE
          Bug off.

Satan places his stack of cash on the small table between them.
Dave is speechless.

                    SATAN
          Use my money and buy a lottery ticket.
          You'll win.

Dave stares at the pile of money and tries not to appear tempted.
He decides to act proud.

                    DAVE
          The lottery? Come on, what do you take me for?

                    SATAN
          A compulsive gambler; a lonely directionless
          human being forever at the mercy of your own
          insignificant hopes and dreams; afraid to admit
          you need love and too weak to accept it when
          it is offered.

Dave glances over at Edie. Satan, seeing this, continues:

                    SATAN
          She pays for your unending coffees herself,
          you know. She doesn't want to cheat the boss.
          She gave you that jacket too.

                    DAVE
          Hey, I found this.

                    SATAN
          You found it on the rack over there.

                    DAVE
          So.

SATAN

She bought it at a flea market in September and
put it there, knowing you would eventually try
and steal it.

Impressed but confounded by all Satan seems to know, Dave
decides to steer the conversation back to practical matters. He
gestures to the cash.

DAVE

What if I win?

SATAN

You keep all the money.

DAVE

That sounds too good to be true.

SATAN

It is.

DAVE
(pretends to be shrewd)
I gotta think about it.

SATAN

Do you believe you have a soul?

DAVE

Who, me?

SATAN

Yeah.

DAVE

No. I have a mind. I have senses. The soul is
only what we call our awareness of things.
But it's really just a material phenomenon.

Satan is intrigued. He sits forward, gesturing to Edie over at the
bar.

SATAN

So, you don't think Edie has a soul either?

Glancing over at his girlfriend, Dave tries to backpeddle.

DAVE

Well not in, you know, that… She's soulful.
Full of soul.

SATAN

So, people don't have souls. It's just something
they acquire from the outside?

DAVE

Yeah. That's it. Sure.

SATAN

People aren't born with souls?

DAVE

No. People—we're material. Mechanisms.
Biological accidents.

Satan backs off. He considers Dave a moment, then:

SATAN

Okay, look: let's say that if you win the lottery
with my money you keep all the cash. But
tonight, when God destroys the world as we
know it, Edie's soul goes to the devil and
remains there for all eternity. Deal?

DAVE
(eerily offended)
Take a powder, creep!

SATAN
(stands)
I'll be back.

Dave watches Satan walk away to the men's room and shivers

with disgust.

DAVE

Lunatic.

But then he looks down at the stack of cash on the table and bites his lip. He grabs a hundred-dollar bill off the top and crosses to the bar.

DAVE
(continues)

Edie, come on. Let's play the lottery. Pick some numbers.

13. INTERIOR, HOTEL MEN'S ROOM—DAY

Satan washes his hands and looks in the mirror. Shifting his gaze, he looks directly at us.

SATAN

Sure, go ahead, call me petty. But one more good soul snatched away from the all-knowing unknowable is still another feather in my cap. So what if it's the last day of the world? I'm not going to give in without a fight, come what may. Let God the Almighty rule eternity; my precincts are the minutes and hours of the everyday. And as long as people have hopes and dreams, well, then, I'll have my work to do.

14. INTERIOR, HOTEL BAR & LOBBY—DAY

Edie pencils in her lottery ticket numbers.

15. EXTERIOR, BOWLING ALLEY—DAY

Jesus and Magdalena step out of a cab and approach.

16. INTERIOR, BOWLING ALLEY—DAY

They enter and walk past the rows of lanes, headed toward an area in back where there are aisles of lockers. Magdalena stands watch as Jesus locates the appropriate locker, number 666. He takes the key the hotel desk clerk gave him and pauses.

JESUS
(voiceover)

I had been there before. Always the same. The
loud and crowded eye of the storm. The brute
unconcerned roar of predestination.

Inserting and twisting the key, he opens the locker and glances up the aisle at Magdalena. She turns and walks away, troubled. Jesus pauses, then reaches inside the locker and retrieves a standard issue laptop computer.

17. INTERIOR, HOTEL LOBBY & BAR—DAY

Satan and Dave continue talking.

DAVE

So, you believe in God, I assume?

SATAN

Unfortunately.

DAVE

And you really believe the world is going to
end tonight?

SATAN

It's prophesied.

And he hands Dave a small, well-worn Bible bookmarked at a certain page. Dave takes it and reads.

DAVE

"Then I saw in the right hand of the one seated
on the throne a book with Seven Seals and I saw
a mighty angel proclaiming with a loud voice:
'Who is worthy to open the book and to break
the seals thereof?'"

                    EDIE

What is a seal?

                    DAVE

It's a—it's like a stamp.

                    SATAN

It sort of keeps the book shut.

                    EDIE

What's written in the book?

                    SATAN

The names of the 144,000 good souls who
will be saved from eternal damnation.

                    DAVE
                (continues reading)
"Then one of the elders said to me, 'Do not weep,
see the lion of the tribe of Judah, the root of
David, has conquered so that he can open the
book and its Seven Seals.'"

                    SATAN

And every time he opens one of those seals
he brings the Apocalypse one step closer.

                    EDIE

Oh, really?

                    SATAN

Seals One through Four: warfare, slaughter,
famine, pestilence. Open a newspaper, see
for yourselves. This is it. It's all over. Three
more to go. Everything I worked so
hard to achieve—wiped out!

He hangs his head, defeated. Dave slaps him on the back.

                    DAVE

You shouldn't take it so hard.

SATAN

I've been misunderstood. They think I hold a
grudge against humanity, but that's not it at all.
I just happen to think that this is a good system;
this tug of war between heaven and hell. It
keeps people honest.

EDIE
(to Dave)
How will I know the winning lottery number?

DAVE
They'll announce it on the radio.

SATAN
What numbers did you pick?

EDIE
Today's date: 12 - 31 - 19 - 99.

SATAN
Excellent.

DAVE
My New Year's resolution is to give up
gambling forever.

EDIE
Really?

DAVE
Yeah.

SATAN
But there isn't going to *be* a new year!

18. EXTERIOR, BOWLING ALLEY—DAY

Magdalena paces back and forth on the sidewalk outside the
bowling alley, smoking a cigarette, checking her wristwatch, and
keeping a lookout.

19. EXTERIOR, BOWLING ALLEY ROOF—DAY

Jesus has found his way to the roof. He finds an out-of-the-way spot and sits with the laptop. He opens it, and taps a few keys. The display reveals an icon of the book with Seven Seals that everyone is talking about. Four of the seals are already undone.

JESUS
(voiceover)
Each one had been painful over the centuries;
the bringing of war, death, famine, then pestilence.
But this one, the Fifth Seal, this was the one I
feared the most.

He reaches out, hesitates, then drags the cursor across to the book icon. Finally, he clicks. The Fifth Seal snaps open. Jesus looks up and around himself. Already, everything seems different. Setting aside the laptop, he stands and moves cautiously across the roof, approaching with trepidation a hungry-looking, pale, skinny, and broken man kneeling in prayer.

JESUS
(voiceover)
When I had opened the Fifth Seal, I saw the
souls of those who had been slaughtered for
the Word of God.

This martyr looks up at Jesus, and Jesus holds his breath.

MARTYR
Sovereign Lord, holy and true, how long will
it be before you judge and avenge our blood
on the inhabitants of the earth?

Jesus tries to think as he slowly approaches the desperate and brutalized man.

JESUS
(voiceover)
It was the darkest hour of a long, dark night of
the soul. The chill center of divine callousness.

What twisted fairy tale had I allowed myself to
be angled up into? What misplaced gratitude
had I believed to be awe?
                (kneels beside the martyr)
Why had I let these souls believe there was
anything other than sacrifice? Why were they
comforted with dreams of vengeance? Why
hadn't I interfered more? Agitated?
Questioned? Revolted? Panicked by both the
legitimacy and the hopelessness of their cries,
I rose to the occasion—and lied.
                (whispers to martyr)
Rest a little longer until the number of your
fellows will be complete, those who will die,
as you yourself have died, for the Word of God.

The martyr seems comforted. Jesus looks up angrily to heaven.

20. EXTERIOR, BOWLING ALLEY—DAY

Jesus slams out through the doors and onto the sidewalk. Dumping the laptop in a public trash can, he strides off down the street in a blind rage. Magdalena drops her cigarette, stunned. She retrieves the laptop and hurries after him. But he's too far along and she loses him in the crowd.

21. INTERIOR, HOTEL LOBBY & BAR—DAY

Dave and Satan are still talking.

                    SATAN
So, if we're all just biological accidents, how
do you explain love?

                    DAVE
Love is a complex of perfectly concrete natural
impulses.

                    SATAN
                (nods)
A survival mechanism.

                    DAVE
Exactly.

                    SATAN
In that case I can understand why you love
Edie. But why does Edie love you?

                    DAVE
Hey, watch it.

                    SATAN
Any purely biological unit attempting to
mechanize its own survival would seem
destined to pass you by. I'm sorry; you're
less than reliable.

                    DAVE
Yeah, well, you can't imagine what that girl
is capable of!

Edie is listening to the radio and jotting down numbers on the
edge of her receipt pad. Satan, meanwhile, continues:

                    SATAN
Oh, I can imagine all too well. That's my
problem: I can imagine everything too well.
A person's capacity for sacrifice; someone's
life ruined by a simple misunderstanding; the
possibility for disaster in just reaching out to
shake someone's hand; the crippling of one's
self-esteem by an overheard remark. How can
I be responsible for all that? Every intimacy
engenders expectation and every expectation
some unknown disappointment. If the world
were only as large as this room, okay, sure,
then I'd be fine. But it's not. The world is
infinite, expansive, and full of possibility. It's
debilitating.

Suddenly, they notice Edie standing there before them looking
amazed.

                    DAVE
                 (concerned)
You okay?

                    EDIE
We won.

                    DAVE
What?

                    EDIE
The lottery. Look.

And she shows him her receipt pad where she has written down
the winning numbers.

                    EDIE
                  (reads)
12 - 31 - 19 – 99.

Terrified, Dave looks at Satan. Satan just smiles sadly and looks
away.

22. INTERIOR, HOTEL KITCHEN—DAY

Satan has somehow organized a news crew to interview Edie as
she works with the hotel kitchen staff to make large quantities of
soup. Dave paces in the hallway, worried.

                   SATAN
              (hosting the show)
So, tell us, Edie, what are you going to do
with all the money you won?

                    EDIE
             (pauses in her work)
Oh, I have a dream. When I first came to
New York, I saw so many homeless people
on the street. And I wanted to make soup.
So, people can be warm, like on this cold,
snowy day…

And she goes on to describe the kind of soup they are making.

23. INTERIOR, LAW OFFICES—DAY

The lawyer is interrogating Magdalena as the receptionist takes shorthand notation.

> LAWYER
> Where is he? What's he plan to do? Who does he think he is, anyway? My client's authority rests on this threat alone! He just can't take things into his own hands and call off the Apocalypse! We can't afford not to go all the way on this thing!

> MAGDALENA
> But he is going all the way. Like at the beginning.

> LAWYER
> Where is the Book of Life?

> MAGDALENA
> *(looks aside and lies)*
> I don't know.

The lawyer looks at the receptionist, pointing to Magdalena:

> LAWYER
> You see! This is what happens when you put responsibility into the hands of amateurs!

> MAGDALENA
> He's willing to forgive, completely!

> LAWYER
> Get her out of here!

The receptionist muscles Magdalena out of the office while the lawyer kicks a wastepaper basket and throws a sheaf of papers in the air. At the door, Magdalena breaks free of the receptionist and runs around a group of desks. The receptionist, though, jumps over a desk, drags open a drawer, and produces a handgun. Meanwhile, the lawyer reappears brandishing a firearm as well. Together, they back Magdalena down the hall and into another office. She's thrown in a seat and—at gunpoint—is forced to confess.

MAGDALENA
The way I remember it, he was on his way to
the Temple. He saw they were throwing stones
at me. He asked them why they were doing this
and they told him what I was.

The receptionist, transcribing again, pauses:

RECEPTIONIST
And what were you?

LAWYER
(interjects)
Adulteress! Whore! Prostitute!

The receptionist decides on something more concise.

RECEPTIONIST
(writing)
Self-employed.

MAGDALENA
He kneeled and looked at the ground. He said,
"Let anyone amongst you who has not sinned
be the first to throw a stone."

LAWYER
(shakes his head)
Typical!

MAGDALENA
He was writing something in the dirt. And he
would not look at me. The people began to
leave; the old people first and then the young.

We were there alone and there was no one
around. I was looking at him but he would not
look at me. He was looking at the ground.
He said, "Where are they? Has no one
condemned you?" And I told him, "No, they're
gone." Then he said, "Neither do I condemn
you. Go your way and from now on do not sin."

                    LAWYER
              (scoffs)
        A likely story!

But the receptionist is on the edge of her seat, deeply moved. The
phone rings and the lawyer answers.

                    LAWYER
          (into phone, listens, then)
        Yeah? Right.
              (hangs up)
        New developments. Let her go. And get me
        Jerusalem on the line.

Magdalena watches the man leave, looks at her recent foe, and
concludes:

                    MAGDALENA
              (of Jesus)
        I thought he had fallen in love with me.

                    RECEPTIONIST
              (sighs)
        He's that kind of guy.

24. INTERIOR, LAW OFFICES LOBBY—DAY

Magdalena rides the elevator down and drifts listlessly through
the lobby towards the street.

25. EXTERIOR, STREETS—DAY

She wanders aimlessly until she comes across—

26. INTERIOR, MUSIC STORE—DAY

Entering, she browses casually before discovering a listening station. She puts on the headphones and searches the database. Finding the song she's after, she presses some numbers and waits. Lost in her private listening and disregarding the loud music playing throughout the store, Magdalena sings aloud:

> MAGDALENA
> Those schoolgirl days
> Of telling tales and biting nails
> Are gone…
> But in my mind
> I know they will still live
> On and on…
>
> But how do you thank someone
> Who has taken you from crayons to perfume?
> It isn't easy but I'll try…
>
> If you wanted the sky I would write
> Across the sky in letters
> A thousand feet high:
> To sir, with love!

27. INTERIOR, BAR—DAY

Later, Magdalena sits alone at the bar and has a martini. Dave enters and approaches, carrying a shallow cardboard box holding a dozen cups of hot soup. He places one on the bar before Magdalena.

> DAVE
> Here, have some hot soup.

> MAGDALENA
> I'm not hungry.

> DAVE
> Yeah, sure, not now. But later… You know
> how it is.

MAGDALENA
You should give it to someone who needs it.

DAVE
We all need to eat. You got a light?

She does. She lights his cigarette and Dave settles down beside
her at the bar. Magdalena is curious about the box of free soup.

MAGDALENA
Do you work for a charity organization?

DAVE
No. This is my girlfriend's idea. She's like,
 you know, terminally good.

MAGDALENA
She'll be remembered.

DAVE
Can I ask you a question?

MAGDALENA
Sure.

DAVE
Do you think the world is going to end
tonight?

MAGDALENA
It might.

DAVE
Do you think God is going to save only the
good souls and send everyone else to hell?

MAGDALENA
(shrugs)
That's what the prophets say.

Dave smokes, considers this, then confesses.

                              DAVE
          I think I gambled away my girlfriend's soul
          to the devil today by accident.

                           MAGDALENA
          Why?

                              DAVE
          It was a long shot. I lost.

                           MAGDALENA
          I'm sorry.

                              DAVE
          Look, how was I supposed to know he was
          the devil? I'm an atheist. They don't teach
          atheists stuff like that!

He lays his head on the bar, distraught. Magdalena hesitates then
comes closer and places her hand on his shoulder.

                           MAGDALENA
          I know someone who will help you.

28. EXTERIOR, STREET—DAY

Jesus comes up out of the subway and approaches a payphone.
But he realizes he has no change. Edie passes by carrying a shallow cardboard box with paper cups of hot soup.

                             JESUS
          Excuse me. Have you got a quarter I can
          borrow for the phone?

Edie gives him some change. Jesus dials and waits for his call to
be answered.

29. INTERIOR, HOTEL LOBBY & BAR—DAY

(Intercut with previous scene) Satan is startled when his cell
phone rings. Pulling it from his pocket, he flips it open and, seeing

the number, hesitates. Finally, he answers.

                    SATAN
    Yeah?

                    JESUS
    It's me. Listen, we have to talk.
              (listens)
    Okay. When? Where? Right. Okay. Bye.

Jesus hangs up. Likewise, Satan switches off his phone, breathless, elated, but uncertain. Jesus, meanwhile, notices Edie again. She is watching him from a few yards away. She approaches and hands him a soup.

                    EDIE
    Are you ok?

                    JESUS
    I think so. Do you work for some charity
    organization or something?

                    EDIE
    No. I'm rich.

                    JESUS
    Really?

                    EDIE
    Yes, very rich. Bye.

And Jesus watches as she walks on and enters the subway.

30. INTERIOR, ANOTHER BAR—DAY

Satan checks his wristwatch and tosses back a shot of vodka. He looks over just as Jesus enters the otherwise abandoned saloon and approaches.

                    SATAN
    This is breaking the rules, you know.

JESUS

I work for the one who makes the rules.

SATAN

Yeah, well, I used to work for him too, until
I quit and started making my own rules.

Jesus sits across from him.

JESUS

You didn't quit. You were fired.

Stung, Satan drinks and pours both himself and Jesus fresh shots.
Jesus tosses back the vodka and lets loose.

JESUS

I won't do it. I refuse.

SATAN

What are you talking about?

JESUS

The Apocalypse.

SATAN

Pull yourself together. You can't do that.

JESUS

Why not?

SATAN
(confounded)
Well, it's… prophesied.

JESUS
(irritated)
I don't give damn about the prophets! I never
liked those guys anyway. We were supposed
to change the world with love, compassion and
forgiveness. This divine vengeance crap is all
wrong!

SATAN
(encouraged)
Are you saying what I think you're saying?

JESUS
I won't judge the living and the dead. I hate
this exclusive, closed-door policy. Who do
these Christians think they are, anyway?

SATAN
My friend, you speak heresy—worse,
revolution!

JESUS
And what's that to you?

SATAN
Well, I have, as it were, merely a professional
interest. If the current state of affairs is to continue,
it would be nice to know you were on my side.

JESUS
That will never happen.

SATAN
You have exiled yourself from paradise.

JESUS
We've allowed a huge misunderstanding to
distort the soul of humanity!

SATAN
We? Hey, look, it wasn't my idea to give
them souls!

JESUS
Without souls they could never have invented
us.

SATAN
That's true. We are their greatest creation.

JESUS

There is no creation without responsibility.

SATAN

Ah, yes. Remember Frankenstein.

JESUS

Faust.

SATAN

Rabbi Loew of Prague.

They toast. Jesus looks down into his glass and sighs.

JESUS

I imagined the truth of the Gospel to be self-
evident. But I had no idea it would be perverted
by the very people who claimed to preach it in
my name.

Satan pours them more vodka and motions to the waitress to bring
another bottle.

SATAN

You shouldn't take it so hard; people just like
to kill each other. It's natural.

JESUS

No, you're generalizing. You can't do that
with these human beings. They're too
complex.

SATAN

(patronizingly)

That's how it starts: the allure of their free will,
the infatuation, the thrill of infinite possibility.
Then, before you know it: wham! You're
addicted to human beings.

JESUS

I admire their persistence.

SATAN

It's amazing the things they get up to. They're
inventing themselves now: artificial
intelligence and cyber genetics and so on.

JESUS

It's impressive, I admit.

SATAN

They're cross-fertilizing pears with apples and
sheep with goats, tobacco plants with lightning
bugs.

JESUS

Now, that's just stupid.

SATAN

I agree, but the potential for synthetically
fabricated organic diseases is too good to
be true. They'll be obsessed with themselves
in entirely new ways now and, frankly, I
think it's about time.
            (then, worried)
I mean, that is, if there is time.

Jesus rubs his forehead and wrestles with his thoughts. He crosses
to another table and sits.

JESUS

There's time.

SATAN
        (relieved)
You sure?

JESUS

There's time for these people to prove you
wrong.

SATAN

I doubt it.

                    JESUS
You always do.

Satan comes over and sits beside him, gripping his little pocket
Bible.

                    SATAN
          Listen, I've got a better idea—as long as you're
          banished from the presence of the most perfect.
          How many seals are left to open?

                    JESUS
                (bored)
          Two.

Satan riffles through the pages of his Bible and finds what he's
looking for.

                    SATAN
                (reads)
          "When he opened the Sixth Seal, I looked and
          there was a great earthquake."
                (inspired)
          Ah, natural disasters! Profitable.

                    JESUS
          It's not that you're so despicable. It's that
          you're so amazingly trite.

                    SATAN
                (unoffended, calculating)
          We can start a new religion!

                    JESUS
          It seems to me to be the last thing these
          people need.

Fed up with Jesus' lack of enthusiasm, Satan stands and paces:

                    SATAN
          What they need and what they want are two

entirely different things. They want divine
retribution and they're willing to pay for it.
I've been in the advertising business since
the beginning, my idealistic young Nazarene.
I'm a pro at telling people what they want to
hear and somehow making them think they've
got to be talked into it. This, you know, it
flatters them. A human being doesn't want to
be anybody's fool.
    (reads from the Bible again)
"The kings, the magnates, the generals, the
powerful of the earth, they hid in the caves
and the rocks of the mountains and called
to the rocks and the mountains, 'Fall on us
and hide us from the wrath of God!'"
    (concedes)
Okay, a little dramatic. But listen, I'm telling
you, that is exactly what will happen. And we
can capitalize on that. Who else are they going
to believe? We'll have the goods to tend their
wounds, nurse their starving children, and
make sense of their suffering in general.
Worldwide, instantaneous, total belief!
    (sits beside Jesus again)
And then, you know, eventually, of course,
they'll be fighting amongst themselves, some
claiming to believe in a better and more
effective way than the others. And a whole
new era of prideful self-assertion will be
ushered in and the innocent will be persecuted
right alongside the guilty. And no one will
know what's right from wrong anymore even
though they…
    (sees Jesus leaving)
Hey! Where are you going?

JESUS

You bore me.

SATAN

Hey, listen, wise guy! You can never go home

again! That's it! We're in the same boat now,
you and me! Sink or swim! You're a man
without a country! An exile!

Jesus pauses, then walks away, worried.

                    JESUS
                 (voiceover)
He was right, as usual. Nothing ever changes.
No one ever learns. I thought maybe the
Apocalypse was a good idea after all.

31. EXTERIOR, STREET—DAY

Satan runs out and catches up with Jesus as he walks away. He
grabs him by the arm.

                    SATAN
Where is it! Where is the Book of Life!

Jesus punches him in the stomach and continues on his way. Satan
falls to his knees. Catching his breath, he stands and addresses us
directly:

                    SATAN
He's a bastard, after all, more human than me,
hard to read. But I can't give up now. I've come
too close. He has a weakness for sacrifice and I
know I can work that angle. I've got to get my
hands on that book!

And he runs off into the city.

32. INTERIOR, HOTEL LOBBY—DAY

Dave drags Edie in from the street and finds Magdalena seated on
a couch across from reception.

                    DAVE
                (makes introductions)
Edie, Magdalena. Magdalena, Edie.

                    EDIE

Hi.

                    DAVE

Edie, Magdalena knows someone who can
help you.

                    EDIE

Do I need help?

                    DAVE

Yes. You're in real big trouble.

                    EDIE

Why?

                    DAVE

I'll explain later.

                    MAGDALENA

He's not here.

                    DAVE

Will he be back?

                    MAGDALENA

I don't know. There's a lot going on. He was
very angry. I've never seen him so mad.

She sits back, distraught. Edie sits beside her and takes her hand,
comfortingly. Dave paces and tries to think of what to do. He sees
Satan watching them from the mezzanine.

                    DAVE

Okay, look, enough with the long faces. Let's
go shopping!

33. INTERIOR, LAW OFFICES—DAY

Jesus walks in past the reception desk. No one is there. The
phones are ringing off the hook. The place is abandoned. He

walks up the hall and passes the receptionist as she runs by with an overstuffed box of documents. Jesus finds the lawyer's office and enters. The lawyer is emptying filing cabinets and preparing to flee. He stops when he sees Jesus.

LAWYER
Ah! Finally: The Son of Man. Sorry, I can't talk right now. We're in a hurry.

JESUS
There's no need to run.

LAWYER
Yeah, that's what you think. The Apocalypse would have been a holiday compared to what's going to happen now that you're a traitor!

JESUS
I'm not a traitor. But I'm not a judge either. Are you yourself so sure you would have been saved?

LAWYER
I cut a deal—a compromise, certainly—but I was saved and I have the documents here somewhere to prove it. Now you've gone and done the unthinkable.

JESUS
I'm sorry. But retribution seems so petty.

LAWYER
I never thought it was a good idea to have a god made flesh. Messy. The human element, you know. Complicated.

JESUS
Has it had no benefits?

The lawyer gestures to the vast panorama out his office window.

LAWYER

That depends on whether what you see out
there is or is not an improvement on imperial
Rome. Personally, I couldn't stomach a
Saturday afternoon at the Colosseum watching
human beings being eaten alive by wild
animals. Yes, I think it's had its benefits. But
it had to be carried through. A threat is a
threat! This change of heart you've suddenly
had—this is a disaster.

The phone rings and he answers.

LAWYER
(continues into phone)
Yeah? What, here? Now? Shit!
(hangs up, to Jesus)
It's the Mormons! I'm outta here! You're on
your own!

He checks the bullets in his gun.

JESUS
Who are the Mormons?

The lawyer shoves Jesus back up against the wall.

LAWYER
Where's the book? What have you done
with it?

JESUS
It's not important.

LAWYER
That's easy for you to say!

JESUS
(pushes back)
I'm fallen now too! Exiled! Further from
God than you yourself!

LAWYER

That doesn't make it any easier for the rest
of us!

JESUS

It was never supposed to be easy!

But now two Mormon thugs are shooting up the office. The
lawyer and the receptionist return fire as Jesus wanders out un-
noticed.

JESUS
(voiceover)

I was the victim of my own history, a pawn
in my father's troubled empire, an insult to
humanity's own godlike self-esteem. I ran
for my life and waited for the walls to come
tumbling down.

34. INTERIOR, HOTEL ROOM—DAY

Dave, Edie, and Magdalena parade happily back into the room
wearing fancy new clothes and carrying champagne and cigars.
They stop, though, when they see Satan lounging comfortably on
the bed waiting for them.

SATAN

Hello, Magdalena.

MAGDALENA

Get your shoes off the bedspread!

He obeys and comes closer.

SATAN

Where is it, Magdalena?

MAGDALENA

I don't know what you're talking about! But
if you're going to hang around, make yourself
useful and open the champagne!

She goes into the bathroom to hide her anger and frustration while
Satan opens the champagne.

                    SATAN
          I talked to your boyfriend today.

                  MAGDALENA
                (rolls her eyes)
            You're so unimaginative.

                    SATAN
          He told me you have the Book of Life.

                  MAGDALENA
          Liar.

Confident and willing to take the time required, Satan turns his
attention to Edie, caressing her cheek.

                    SATAN
          Hello, Edie.

                    EDIE
          Are you really the devil?

                    SATAN
          Yes, I am.

                    EDIE
          Would you like some soup?

Her complete lack of fear or distrust stymies the archfiend and he
looks to Dave for an explanation.

                    DAVE
          She's a Buddhist.

The suite's door opens and Dave jumps to his feet.

                    DAVE
          That him?

SATAN

Relax.

Jesus enters and sees them all. He is immediately and profoundly exhausted. Dave comes forward, starstruck.

DAVE

Hello, my name is Dave and—first of all—I'd just like to apologize for my entire existence.

Jesus gently pushes past him and collapses on the bed. They all gather around him, everyone talking at once.

SATAN

Give me the Book of Life!

MAGDALENA

Don't do it!

DAVE

He's got Edie's soul!

JESUS

Who's Edie?

DAVE
(indicates)

She is.

EDIE
(bows)
Konnichiwa.

Desperate for space, Jesus climbs off the bed and takes refuge in the bathroom. Magdalena follows.

MAGDALENA
(of Edie and Dave)
I thought you might be able to help them.

He throws open a door at the opposite end of the bathroom and escapes to the outer suite. They all follow. He sits on the couch and holds his head in his hands as they descend upon him again.

> JESUS
>
> Let go of Edie's soul and I'll give you the book.

> MAGDALENA
>
> No!

> SATAN
>
> It's a deal!

> JESUS
>
> Give it to him.

Reluctantly, Magdalena produces the laptop from where she has hidden it in her backpack. She hands it to Satan. Relieved, Dave claps Jesus on the shoulder as he goes to pour the champagne.

> DAVE
>
> Thanks, man. That was close.

> JESUS
>
> Don't mention it.

> MAGDALENA
> *(despondent)*
>
> This is a mistake. He'll just make things worse!

> SATAN
>
> Yes, it's a tragedy. But it's a beautiful thing nevertheless. It doesn't get any better than this.

> JESUS
>
> It doesn't get any worse either.

> SATAN
>
> We'll see.

Satan exits. Magdalena collapses on the bed.

> MAGDALENA
Oh! What have I done!

Jesus falls back on the couch and catches his breath.

> JESUS
> *(voiceover)*
I was changing fast. Addicted, perhaps, to humanity.

35. EXTERIOR, HOTEL—NIGHT

Satan exits the hotel. But he can't seem to open the Book of Life laptop. James, the homeless man with binoculars we first met at the airport, is passing by.

> SATAN
> *(stops James)*
Hey you! You know anything about computers?

> JAMES
A little.

> SATAN
Open this thing for me, will you. I've got… arthritis.

James struggles with the laptop too as Satan tries to flag down a taxi. Finally, James gives up.

> JAMES
Sorry, there seems to be some sort of a lock on it.

> SATAN
> *(frustrated)*
Give me that thing!

He yanks the laptop from James and gets in a taxi.

36. INTERIOR, COMPUTER REPAIR SHOP—NIGHT

A line of people with busted computers trails the length of the store, out the door, and onto the sidewalk. Satan disregards everyone and strides directly up to the overworked repairman at his workbench.

> SATAN
>
> I need this thing opened.

> REPAIRMAN
>
> Sir, there's a line.

> SATAN
>
> Open it.

> REPAIRMAN
>
> We don't service that brand.

> SATAN
>
> That's not what it says on the sign outside.

> REPAIRMAN
>
> It's a foreign manufacturer.

> SATAN
>
> How foreign?

> REPAIRMAN
>
> Egyptian.

> SATAN
>
> Old?

> REPAIRMAN
>
> Ancient. And its warranty is expired. Next!

37. EXTERIOR, COMPUTER REPAIR SHOP—NIGHT

Satan shuffles back out to the sidewalk. He looks up and down the street, adjusts his collar and shoots his cuffs before addressing us:

                    SATAN
Who said it first, "Childlike innocence is not
a viable alternative to despair"?
          (shakes his head, sighs)
Those bastards in heaven, they've thought of
everything.

A car horn toots and he looks over to find the lawyer leaning out
the window of a taxi. He looks desperate. The receptionist runs
around the back of the taxi, still hectically organizing loose
paperwork.

                    LAWYER
              (of laptop)
Is that it?

                    SATAN
              (approaches)
Back off, pal.

                    LAWYER
Listen, I know that with recent developments
no one can be sure of anything. It's a volatile
time. Only the fittest will survive this period
of transition.

                    SATAN
Yeah, yeah, yeah. What are you getting at?

                    LAWYER
It's my professional opinion that at this crucial
juncture in your career you need serious legal
counsel of the kind only someone with my
expertise can provide.

Unimpressed, Satan leans back against the taxi and gives the
receptionist the once-over. She has great legs and enjoys the effect
she's having on the prince of darkness.

                    SATAN
Are you with him?

RECEPTIONIST

That depends.

Satan straightens his tie and offers his arm to the young woman.

SATAN

Come on.

She dumps the paperwork into the lawyer's taxi and goes off with Satan. Shaking his head, the lawyer polishes his glasses and barks at the driver

LAWYER

The airport! Quick!

38. EXTERIOR, NEW YORK CITY—NIGHT

It's New Year's Eve. Crowds of people everywhere are celebrating and enjoying themselves.

JESUS
(voiceover)

And the new year arrived, the new millennium.

39. INTERIOR, HOTEL ROOM—NIGHT

Jesus and company are partying extravagantly.

JESUS
(voiceover)

Just another day in a lifetime of similar days…

Satan arrives with the receptionist and tosses the laptop aside, resigned. Dave pours champagne and the receptionist starts dancing wildly.

JESUS
(voiceover)

But each day crowded with possibility, the

possibility of disaster and the possibility of
perfection.

Later, Edie, Magdalena, and Satan have their arms over each
other's shoulders, singing.

JESUS
(voiceover)

To be there amongst them was good; the
innocent and the guilty, all equally helpless,
all perfectly lost, and, as frightening as it was
to admit, all deserving of forgiveness.

40. EXTERIOR, STATEN ISLAND FERRY—DAY

Dave, Edie, Magdalena, Satan, and the receptionist, are finishing
their night of partying aboard the ferry as it pulls out of lower
Manhattan and into New York Harbor. Jesus sits off by himself,
watching them.

JESUS
(voiceover)

What would become of them, I wondered. In
another hundred years would they all be born
in test tubes? Or perhaps evolve through
computers to become groups of disembodied
digital intelligence machines? Would they
believe in me? Would they remember me?
Would they remember what I said? Would it
matter?

As they sip coffee from paper cups and chat about little things,
Jesus wanders out to the back of the ferry with the laptop. He
throws it into the harbor and watches it sink.

JESUS
(voiceover)

In a hundred years would they be living on
other planets? Would they outgrow war?
Would the earth still exist? Would they
engineer themselves genetically so that

disease was thing of the past? Would they all just become one big multiethnic race? Would they discover the secret of the universe? God? Would they become gods themselves? What will they eat? Will they make love? Maybe there will be more than two sexes. Will they be lonely? Will they still believe life is sacred? Will it matter? Did we matter?

The End ~

Soon

Seven performers enter the stage, four men and three women. They are carrying the few props they will use; a footstool, a Bible, and four short boompoles with microphones attached. They will use these throughout the performance to mic themselves and each other. It is clear they have done this before and consider it a chore. Jed sets the footstool downstage center and Eve lays the Bible upon it, open. Gus and Lea quarrel wordlessly over which of them should have a mic. Lea finally relinquishes it and goes over to join Jed and Eve kneeling in prayer. Meanwhile, Bob stands off to the side, staring at the floor, despondent, while Meg gazes up into the rafters in a mixture of horror and fascination. Tom, however, is fixated on the Bible. Standing a few yards away from it, his finger raised, a question on his lips, he hesitates. Gus then raises the mic to the man's mouth and they begin.

TOM

(recites)
See how I burn in my love, how hungrily
I long.

All is still, silent and suspended. But the spell is broken when Tom leans back, takes the mic from Gus and discourses learnedly in a confident and relaxed manner. The women listen, half in love with him.

TOM

So is the lover's soul consumed with
indescribable fire, shot through with the
flames of heavenly light. There is no end
to this fervor and happiness as I push on
towards the object of my love. Death
becomes sweet to me as well as sure.

He hands the mic to Bob and wanders away, further upstage, lost in the beauty of these ideas. Skeptical, Bob watches him go, then turns downstage and pursues his own troubled thoughts.

BOB

What is it?
This feeling
This impulse

This willingness to admit
Life, history, this self-consciousness
I cannot help but call reality
Is no mistake
Or accident.

What is it, then
I feel confirmed in the exquisite but overlooked
Patterns of the everyday?
A willingness to admit,
Or confess
I am not worthy to know all
Or nothing?

I confess I suspect I want
To believe
And doubt,
Since I wonder if I can
Really
Subordinate my reason
To the needs of my soul.

We do not know
And fear to follow so invent
Faith
To call our own and God's
Mercy.

Still, the fact remains
We exist and are always
Disappointed
By ourselves
We construct and discover
Devise and illuminate
But are rarely brought further
Than the limits of the life
We ourselves
Construct and discover
Devise and illuminate.
And so on.
I want to believe!

                    JED
Then pray.

                    BOB
I can't pray without proof.

                    GUS
Of what?

                    BOB
God's plan. There has got to be a system.
I'm sure there is a method.

Meanwhile, the women are dreamily grooving on Tom's initial
recitation, trying out the quotation for themselves.

                    MEG
See how I burn… how I… See…

                    LEA
How hungrily I… Long… How hungrily…

                    EVE
Love, see how I burn, how I long…

Losing patience, Bob turns away to Gus and Jed.

                    BOB
We must do something!

                    TOM
                 (suggests)
God wants us to live in the world, not in
spite of it.

                    LEA
                  (adds)
Yes, we earn grace.

                    BOB
No! We are given grace.

GUS
(threatened)
And so what! So what if we are given grace?
So what if there is nothing we can do to earn it?
Is that supposed to change the way we feel,
the way we live—the way we die?

BOB
Yes!

MEG
But why?

BOB
Do you believe in the infallibility of scripture?

MEG
Of course.

BOB
Good. So do I. But I want to know how it works.

LEA
All will be revealed in time.

BOB
But to whom? And how long is time, anyway?

EVE
That is God's business.

LEA
His ways are not known to man.

BOB
Yes, but that is not God's fault, is it? It's ours.
(as they appear shocked)
Look! There is an end to time. And a clearly
stated sequence of events heralding its
approach. It's here, in the Bible. We were
meant to know this!

                    JED
We were meant to abide.

                    BOB
But by what! Look! Either there is justice or
there is not. Either there will be a final
judgment or not. The prophecies are either
true or… well, false. God must be as angry
and as dissatisfied as I am! I'm sure of it!
Look around you! The signs are everywhere!

                    TOM
The signs?

                    MEG
What signs?

                    JED
Signs of what?

                    BOB
The Apocalypse! The millennium! The
glorious last gasp of history, human and
otherwise! If this is not the end of the world
as promised in the Bible, then my trust in the
good book, my faith in God, and the small
measure of self-respect I allow myself, are—
well, finished.

                    GUS
Sir, please, you are a fanatic.

                    BOB
No! Look! I've done the math!
          (riffles through the pages)
The Book of Daniel in the Old Testament,
chapter nine, verse twenty-four, predicts that
seventy weeks shall pass from, "the going
forth of the commandment to restore and
rebuild Jerusalem until an anointed one shall
be cut off and be killed."

GUS

But the seventy weeks came and went, wise
guy, and nothing ever happened.

JED

(tries to impress the girls)
The "going forth of the commandment" refers,
of course, to King Cyrus the First of Persia
who sent the Israelite, Ezra, back to rebuild the
Temple in Jerusalem in 457 BC.

But the girls are not impressed and push past Jed to hear Tom,
who is intrigued with Bob's ideas.

TOM

Nevertheless, my friend, there is still no
mention anywhere in the Old Testament that
seventy weeks later an anointed one appeared
and was or was not killed.

BOB

Maybe. But look, here, in Ezekiel, chapter
four, verse six…

The Bible is thrust into Lea's hands and she reads:

LEA

"You shall lay down a second time and bear
the punishment of the house of Judah; forty
days I assign you, one day for each year."

BOB

What happens if we apply Ezekiel's equation
of a day for every year to the seventy weeks
of Daniel's prophecy?

TOM

Seventy weeks is 490 days.

BOB

But if those 490 days were 490 years and we

began counting forward from "the going forth of the commandment to restore and rebuild Jerusalem," that would be—what?

                    TOM
490 years from the year 457 BC…

                    BOB
Brings us to…

                    JED
Thirty-three.

                    TOM
AD.

                    BOB
33 AD. The very year Jesus Christ was crucified and died on the cross at Golgotha.

                    EVE
          (blinks)
Wow.

                    TOM
          (admits)
We're impressed.

                    GUS
          (skeptical)
By your math.

                    BOB
If the Bible predicts—to within the year—the crucifixion of the Messiah, why ignore its predictions about the Second Coming? The Apocalypse? The millennium? In chapter eight, verse fourteen, Daniel speaks of a period of, "2,300 days which shall pass before the sanctuary shall be cleansed." Now, what can this mean?

GUS
(fed up)
Anything!

JED
(shoves him)
Use your imagination!

BOB
Twenty-three hundred days figured not as
days, but as years.

TOM
Two thousand three hundred years from the
year 457 BC brings us to…

Suspense. Everyone's counting on their fingertips. Finally, one by
one, they all reach the same conclusion. They fall silent and tense.
Lea, amazed, lowers herself to her knees and calls out:

LEA
Now!

The date 1843 is projected onto the stage as all of them collapse in
various postures of prayer.

BOB
Finding all the signs of the times and the
present condition of the world to compare
harmoniously with the prophetic descriptions
of the last days, I am compelled to believe
that the world has, indeed, reached the limits
of its continuance. I need not speak of the joy
that fills my heart in view of this delightful
prospect, nor of the ardent longing of my
soul for a participation in the joys of the
redeemed!

So now everyone is kneeling again, waiting for something to happen. They have been waiting a long time. No one wants to appear
less devout than anyone else, but they're all struggling with bore-

dom. Finally, Eve, the youngest of the crowd, gets up quietly and walks over to Jed.

EVE

Is it happening?

JED

No.

EVE

When?

JED

Soon. Go back and pray.

EVE

How will we know?

JED

What?

EVE

When it happens.

JED

Are you stupid or what? There will be signs. The world will go up in flames. We'll all be taken up to heaven and live forever in perfect peace and happiness.

EVE

Yeah, but… Like, for instance, how do you know you'll be saved and taken up to heaven?

JED
(offended)

What are you trying to say?

EVE

Only a small number of people will go to heaven.

195

                    JED
Oh yeah? How many?

                    EVE
One hundred and forty-four thousand. It says
so in the Bible.

                    JED
All over the world?

                    EVE
That's what it says.

She shows him the page in the book. He takes it from her. Meg
has been listening. Now she comes closer.

                    MEG
Throughout all of history?

                    EVE
               (shrugs)
I think so.

Jed stands and approaches Tom, who has been overhearing all this
and preparing himself for trouble. Jed points out the passage.

                    JED
Is this true?

                    TOM
          (takes Bible and reads)
"Do not damage the earth or the sea or the
trees until we have marked the servants of
our God… And I heard the number of those
that were sealed… One hundred and
forty-four thousand."

Jed is crushed. He wanders away, scratching his head.

                    JED
How can this be? All my life I have struggled

to be a good Christian. Isn't that worth
anything? I have resisted temptation. I've
fought my violent nature, struggled to be
charitable. How can this be?

Bob tries to console Jed in spite of his own fears.

                    BOB
Come. Kneel in prayer and trust in our Savior.

                    GUS
              (sarcastic)
His math is infallible.

                    TOM
Hey! God will not forsake a good man!

                    GUS
               (scared)
But are there really so few good men? I mean,
and if there are, how is it possible that I can
be one of them? I was reckless in my youth—
depraved even.

                    BOB
              (desperate)
Your efforts towards goodness will not go
unseen! Be consoled in the knowledge that
this imperfect world is about to be
extinguished and a new world begun! The
ways of God, surely, are not known to man.
But the ways of man must, certainly, be
known to God. We hope. We believe. We
think.

But no one is convinced. Tom hands the Bible off to someone else
and comes downstage center, massaging his temples.

                    TOM
And nothing happens.
          (as they all wander away)

How profound our disappointment.
How cold our isolation.
How desperate and lonely now the universe
    appears
To us
The faithful
In these, the final days.
                (looks up, hopeful)
But!

                        MEG
Then!

                        BOB
Later!

Eve begins shaking all over, having some sort of ecstatic experience.

                        TOM
Is she all right?

                        JED
It's a miracle!

                        GUS
Knock it off!

Eve's fit stops all of a sudden and she stands there on her toes,
gazing up into the overhead lights.

                        EVE
Heaven opened up and I saw the world
beneath me and the fields and the streams of
heaven made a beautiful sound and the angels
were singing and they told me to wait and to
live in hope for Jesus has come down to us—
but he is waiting!

                        JED
Where?

                              EVE

Outside!

                              JED

Outside where?

                              EVE

Outside the sanctuary!

                              JED

What sanctuary?

                              EVE

In the Temple!

                              JED

But where is the Temple?

Meg, seeing an opportunity to rekindle their enthusiasm, grabs
Jed's mic and waves him away.

                              MEG

It's a metaphor, you idiot! Look, Christ is
outside, in the doorway or… the outer hall or
the… How do you say?

                              BOB

Vestibule?

                              TOM

Foyer!

                              GUS

Porch.

                              MEG
                     (free associating)
He's begun something. Something big.
Something important he has to do first before
descending to earth to judge the living. And in
the meantime, he's begun the ah… The ah…

                    TOM
                (suggests)
The investigative judgment of the dead?

                    MEG
Exactly!

                    BOB
And, of course, we understand that this can
take some time.

                    GUS
                (lawyerly)
It is, as it were, a necessary prerequisite and
so on, etcetera.

                    JED
Justice prevails! Righteousness will be
rewarded! The innocent will be vindicated!

                    MEG
        (with fiery righteousness)
Fallen! Fallen is Babylon! Come out of her
my people, so that you do not take part in her
sins, and so that you do not share in her
plagues; for her sins are heaped as high as
heaven, and God has remembered her
inequities!

They drag Eve forward and sit her down on the footstool, gather-
ing around to grill her on the authenticity of her revelation.

                    EVE
                (meek, careful)
The Temple of God was open in heaven and I
was shown the ark of the covenant. Two
angels stood on either side of it. Jesus raised
the cover of the ark. And I saw the stones on
which the Commandments were written. The
Fourth Commandment was in the center, with
a light surrounding it.

                    BOB
The Fourth Commandment, quick!

                    TOM
                  (reads)
"Remember the Sabbath, and keep it holy."

                    BOB
Ah! You see! It's obvious! We're supposed to
be observing the Sabbath from sundown on
Friday till sundown on Saturday.

                    GUS
               (suspicious)
Wait a minute!

                    MEG
Like the ancient Jews!

                    BOB
Next question!

                    GUS
The Fourth Commandment in the middle of a
list of ten? How is this possible?
                 (to Eve)
How many tablets were there?

                    LEA
               (interjects)
Two.

                    GUS
I'm asking her!

                    EVE
               (uncertain)
Two?

                    JED
There are always two!

                    GUS
The Fourth Commandment, in the middle of a
list of ten, distributed onto more than one
tablet. Think about it: there would have to be
more than two tablets.

                    TOM
             (does the math)
Seven, to be exact. Seven tablets.
Commandments one through four on one
tablet each, and Commandments five through
ten spread out amongst three others.

                    GUS
See what I mean? You ever seen a picture of
Moses carrying around seven tablets?

                    JED
             (confused)
But… there are always two.

                    LEA
Unless…

Hopeful glances in all directions, everyone is grasping for unex-
pected interpretive associations.

                    BOB
Yes, unless…

                    TOM
Easy!

                    JED
She's been given a vision of the true law!
Seven tablets! Not two!

                    MEG
             (entrepreneurial)
You see, this is the kind of thing we could
organize a new church around.

                           TOM
What, like the First Church of the Seven
Tablets?

                           MEG
You know what I mean.

                           GUS
This is crazy!

Meanwhile, Jed, bubbling over with some strange new enthusiasm
all his own, lectures the others on the phenomenon of their friend,
Eve.

                           JED
Notice: the word of God manifesting itself as
a dense electromagnetic field around and
about the head and shoulders of the girl issues
forth in a sort of radiophonic force field
which phases out its own sound waves and
leaves only the visual impression of the
heavenly transcendent.

                           LEA
What are you implying?

                           JED
She's a radio.

Lea smacks him in the back of the head and takes his mic. Taking
charge.

                           LEA
                  (cocks her thumb upstage)
Scram.

Eve runs away and Lea is left watching Gus, who is bent over,
holding his head and looking ill.

                           LEA
Now, what's wrong with you?

GUS

I have received a vision—a revelation.

MEG

Oh yeah? From who?

GUS

Well… God, I guess.
		(corrects himself)
Actually, they were angels. Angels of the
Lord spoke to me. But without words.

BOB

What did these "angels of the Lord" look like?

GUS

They were beautiful—I mean in a sort of
unspeakable kind of way: young, but wise,
chaste, though somehow knowing.

LEA

And what kinds of things did these beautiful
young women tell you?

GUS

They were *angels* of the Lord!

BOB

We'll be the judges of that!

MEG

Sluts, I'm sure. I know the type.

GUS

They gave me instructions.

LEA

About what?

GUS

The Apocalypse.

Excited, they gather around him, eager for details.

GUS
(continues)
The millennium will not be a period of unending
happiness that is going to happen in heaven.
It will happen right here.

LEA

Heretic!

MEG
My friend, you are mistaken. The earth is to
be destroyed and history ended. That is our
salvation, our only hope.

GUS
No, we are to prepare for the Messiah's return
so that we can create a heaven on earth.

TOM
On what authority are we to accept this
revelation of yours?

JED
Yeah. We've already got a prophet and she
says God told her the Messiah's coming back
to destroy this world.

EVE
(the current prophet, bravely)
But surely, we can expect other prophets to
come along as time goes on? Right?

LEA
(patronizing)
Of course, dear, but not like him.

MEG
(leads the girl away)
He's somehow altogether just not the type.

                    GUS

Why is she the only one allowed to have
visions from God?

                    BOB

Her powers of revelation have been verified.

                    GUS

By who?

                    BOB

Well… by us.

                    GUS

How?

They look around at one another, trying to elect someone confident enough to refute him. Lea gives it a shot.

                    LEA

By the belief her visions inspire in us and the
rest of the congregation. What further proof
is needed? Faith sustained is the only measure
of truth. Faith alone is what counts.

The others are very impressed.

                    TOM

Very good.

                    GUS

Oh, I see! It's all about style! I get it. It's all
about a convenient, easy to use, and well
rubbed common consensus; a popular notion
of the look and feel of holiness. Yes, of course,
you can slip into your religion like a tight new
pair of blue jeans and feel utterly invincible.
Fine! My faith, it seems, is not so comfortable;
my God far from reassuring.

Though the others remain unmoved, Eve comes over and lays her hand on his shoulder.

                              EVE
     I'm sorry.

                              GUS
     Forgive me.

A moment of silence. Then they all relax and fall out of character.

                              TOM
                        (takes charge)
     Okay, that's that. Go over there and pretend
     to be somebody else.

                              EVE
                         (annoyed)
     Like who, for instance?

                              JED
                        (passing by)
     Look, don't start! Here, gimme that.

He takes Eve's mic and moves off, eager to move things along.

                              TOM
     Be like a family or something.

                              MEG
                        (delighted)
     That's good! A family! I'm the daughter. You
     be the mother.

                              LEA
     Why am I always the mother?

                              BOB
     Come on! Let's get on with this.

They form a little family unit upstage with Bob as the father and
Jed as the son. Tom joins Gus downstage where he sits brooding.

                                TOM
What now, boss?

                                GUS
Talk to them.

                                TOM
What do I say?

                                GUS
Tell them the truth.

Tom is now a young novice preacher, uncertain of his abilities.

                                TOM
You mean, about, you know—?

                                GUS
Yes. Go ahead!

Tom crosses to center stage and addresses the family.

                                TOM
                           (clumsily)
The day of judgment is at hand.

The family just looks at him, uncomprehending.

                                GUS
And?

                                TOM
People must repent and join the faithful.

                                GUS
And what are the faithful going to do?

Tom turns aside and answers Gus directly.

                                TOM
Well, ah, they're going to overthrow the

armies of Babylon and—

GUS

(impatient)

Don't tell me! Tell them!

Tom turns back to the family and composes himself.

TOM

They're going to overthrow the armies of
Babylon and start a new and better kind of
world.

JED

Dad, what is Babylon?

A stern mother, Lea raises her hand and Jed flinches. Meanwhile,
Meg is a sixteen-year-old coquette flirting with the tongue-tied
young preacher man.

MEG

Where is this new and better world supposed
to be?

TOM

Um—excuse me?

MEG

Where is it? Where is this new and better
world supposed to be?

LEA

(calls)

Are they alone?

MEG

(back over her shoulder)

There's two of them.

JED

Ask them who the armies of Babylon are!

BOB
Just ignore them and they'll go away.

Tom confers with Gus, then returns to Meg.

TOM
Yes.

MEG
Yes, what?

TOM
It will be a new and better world.

MEG
Yes, I know that. But where? Where will this
new and better world be?

TOM
Right here.

MEG
(to the family)
He says it'll be right here.

LEA
Stop teasing them. They're liable to do
something uncivilized.

MEG
(obeying, to Tom)
Sorry, I have to go now.

Gus can stand this no longer. He grabs the mic from Tom and
jumps up on the footstool, towering above them all, very charismatic.

GUS
I'm here to gather an army!

Everyone stops and waits, wordlessly, for more. But the son asks:

JED
Who are the armies of Babylon?

GUS
The armies of Babylon are all around you,
son! The faithless hordes forever at the mercy
of their insatiable desires; the fat cats in the
skyscrapers and down in the stock market pit,
determining the value of other people's lives!
The politicians who hire the police to enforce
the laws designed to keep the good man down!
I say to you now and I will say to anyone
who will listen: Put aside your empty and
damaged lives, walk away from your squalid
and despairing communities, and help do the
work that needs to be done to change this
world into a Garden of Eden! Join God's
army! Join the ranks of the 144,000 faithful
who will fight side by side with the Messiah
when he returns to earth. We will be *his*
people!

Meg falls to her knees, suddenly and passionately converted.

MEG
We will live like the first Christians! Like the
apostles! A community built upon mutual
need and charity, secure in our appointed duty
towards God!

TOM
(confused)
So, are we like—communists now?

A major faux pas. Everything falls silent. Tom flinches and backs
away, terrified, as Gus focuses his fury on him alone. The date
1950 is projected on the floor.

GUS
Hey! I fought in the war under the flag of
this great nation of ours! I defended

democracy in trenches knee-deep with the
blood of my best friends! I caught a bullet in
the right temporal lobe and recovered just in
time to recite the Beatitudes to a troop of
panicked teenagers, moments before they
froze to death on a night no one else even
remembers! This great nation of ours was
founded by a religious community not so
different than our own and you can come out
here and call me whatever you like! But don't
ever—don't *ever*—call me a communist!

Stirred by the oratory, the congregation begins reciting their own peculiar pledge of allegiance, like students in a classroom.

ALL
As Christian students in these, the final days,
we pledge our hearts and minds, our hands,
our all, to the flag of God's eternal kingdom,
and to the theocracy for which it stands, one
people made up of all nations, and bound by
the cords of everlasting love, liberty, purity,
justice, peace, happiness and life for all!

They all take their places, sitting obediently on the floor as their teacher, Gus, paces back and forth with the Bible.

GUS
There will be another. Another Christ.
Another Messiah.

LEA
What about Jesus?

GUS
He didn't fulfill all the prophecies.

EVE
He died for our sins.

He has anticipated this. He nods and comes closer.

GUS

Yes, of course. But he didn't get married and have children, now, did he? Look, Psalm 45 tells us how a *King* is to be anointed and ride triumphantly on a *white horse*, and he will have many *arrows*. The *King* represents the Messiah and the *arrows* represent his children. Is this not obvious?

JED

You mean…?

GUS
(slams the book)
Yes! The King, when he arrives, will not be some monk locked up in a cloister, but a man of the world having, as it were, a way with the women. The Book of Revelation corroborates this when it describes the Apocalypse: "I looked and there was a white horse!" See? "Its rider had a bow and a crown was given to him."
(turns to class)
Now, who wears a crown?

JED

A king.

GUS

Good. And what's a king likely to use a bow for?

JED

To shoot.

GUS

To shoot what?

JED
(eager)
Women!

                    GUS
              (sighs)
No.

                    BOB
Arrows.

                    GUS
Right! And what will the arrows do?

They're all lost, but Eve takes a stab at it.

                    EVE
Make babies?

                    GUS
Exactly! Make babies!

Gus throws up his arms in triumph. The class disperses. Gradually, he sinks to the floor and appears old and tired. Meg comes down over him.

                    GUS
I'm dying.

                    MEG
              (scared)
You can't! The Messiah has not arrived yet!

                    GUS
I know. I've failed. But you'll succeed. You must become the new prophet.

                    MEG
I don't want to.

                    GUS
You're the only one I trust.

                    MEG
But I do not have the gift of prophecy.

GUS

It'll come to you when you need it.

MEG

(piously)

I am not worthy.

GUS

(annoyed)

Get worthy! Someone must become for these people a lens to focus their various hopes and dreams into one bright beam of light. That light will be seen. Someone will come. And you'll know him when you see him.

MEG

But will they believe me?

GUS

They will believe you if what you tell them is the truth.

MEG

How will I know if it is the truth?

GUS

The faithful will know the truth when they see it.

And he dies. Meg is worried, threatened. The others approach.

LEA

What now?

MEG

(defensive)

What do you mean by that?

LEA

(uncertain)

I mean…

BOB

She means…
> *(equally uncertain, to Lea)*

What do you mean?

LEA

Our prophet is dead! What do we do now?

JED

> *(to Meg)*

You know something, don't you?

Meg moves aside, panicking, as the community's desire for signs and meanings accelerates.

MEG

Go away. Leave me alone!

BOB

Don't panic!

They corner Meg, pressing in close. Reluctantly, she admits:

MEG

He said I should keep my eyes open.

LEA

For what?

MEG

Signs.

JED

Ah! You see, she knows something!

LEA

You're the new prophet, admit it!

MEG

> *(falls back)*

No! I'm not! Really!

BOB

Don't try and hide it!

JED

Why would he have given you instructions if
he didn't think you were a prophet?

Trapped, she answers as honestly as she can.

MEG

Because—he loved me.

Confirmed in their suspicion, the others apprehend Meg, forcing
her to lie face down on the floor. They place the footstool astride
her and Lea steps up onto it.

LEA

You have not suffered. You have not yet
earned your revelations. It is our duty to help
you transcend. To discipline your austerities.
To focus your attention more perfectly upon
the divine.

Meanwhile, Gus, lying forgotten upstage, gets up and crosses
down to Meg, ignored by the others. He stomps his foot to get her
attention, then places the Bible on the floor and points to it.

GUS

Seven!

He then runs around and becomes part of the congregation.

LEA
(continues her speech)
Think not that we torment you in anger. Your
suffering we keep before us at all times and
we pray for your deliverance.

MEG
(humble)
Excuse me.

                    LEA
Yes?

                    MEG
The prophet appeared to me.

                    LEA
When?

                    MEG
Just now.

They all come down close to the floor to interrogate her.

                    LEA
What did he say?

                    MEG
He stomped his foot, called out the number
seven, and pointed to an open page of the
Bible.

                    JED
          (off to the side, pointing)
You mean… this Bible?

They jump up, startled and apprehensive.

                    LEA
Don't touch it!

                    BOB
          (approaches bravely)
Stand back!
          (reads)
"One thousand two hundred and sixty days
shall pass during which the Lord will allow
his two witnesses to prophesy."

                    LEA
Two witnesses? That's new.

BOB

"And there will be a period of forty-two
months during which the nations will
overrun the Holy City."

JED

One thousand two hundred and sixty days is
forty-two months.

BOB

Though, of course, that could mean years.

EVE

Or weeks.

BOB

So, forty-two months plus one thousand two
hundred and sixty days equals eighty-four
months.

JED

Or seven years.

BOB

Exactly.

EVE

A holy number!

LEA

Oh my God! She really is a prophet! Get her
up out of there!

They lift the footstool up and away and help Meg to her feet.

BOB

But who is it? Who is the other witness the
Lord will allow to prophesy?

MEG

I will know him when I see him.

LEA
(encouraging)
Yes, and for seven years the two of you will
prophesy and make the way straight for the
Messiah's return!

MEG
(careful)
Apparently.

BOB
Though, of course, there's this bit here about
the Holy City being overrun in the meantime.

MEG
The prophet, when he arrives, will be able to
explain that. For now, wait. Wait and pray.

They scatter and kneel in prayer while Meg hopes for the best and
and tries to appear confident. Jed is now the troubled and dissatisfied son of the prophetess. He fidgets as the others pray. Tom
approaches the congregation now as a newcomer. The year 1978
is projected on the floor.

JED
(to Tom)
What do you think?

TOM
I'm new around here.

This excites Jed. He sidles over on his knees. Meg has noticed the
newcomer too and he, in turn, has noticed her.

JED
That's what we need around here! New blood.
New ideas! I've had some myself, you know.
Ideas, I mean. But I keep quiet about them.
You know how people are. They misunderstand
everything. One day, though, when my
experiments are complete—

                              MEG
Silence!

                              JED
Wait! No. It's my mother. Okay. Shut up.
Kneel. Pray.

Tom kneels with the others, all the while keeping his eyes trained
on Meg far downstage.

                              TOM
What are we praying for?

                              LEA
                  (jumps up, hysterical)
Justice!

She passes out and falls into Gus' arms. He lays her down gently.
Meg speaks aloud to herself and only Tom hears her.

                              MEG
And still nothing happens.
How profound our disappointment
How cold this isolation
How desperate and lonely now the universe appears
   again
To us
The faithful
In these the final days.

Eve has prayed herself into a kind of trance.

                              EVE
See how I burn in my… burn in my love…
in my love how hungrily… how hungrily I
long…

                              MEG
                  (to Tom, of the congregation)
The sincerity of their need convinces me. And
the constancy of their devotion replenishes

my own. Their belief itself guides me and the
Word of God is revealed for their benefit. I
believe I do the Lord's bidding. Though, I do
not know how. Is that wrong?

Tom rises to his feet, calm, assured, and charismatic.

> TOM
> You keep faith alive in them.

> MEG
> But I can hardly believe the things I hear
> myself say.

> TOM
> The truth of revelation depends on the amount
> of faith available. Without a sufficient number
> of faithful, the prophecies are meaningless. If
> you stumble from time to time in your
> understanding, you do add to God's people
> and help prepare the world to hear the truth
> when it comes.

As they speak, they come closer to one another and finally em-
brace like lovers. Jed moves about and watches from the sidelines,
suspicious.

> MEG
> You are an interesting young man, well suited
> to the times, I think.

> JED
> Mother, come away from the stranger.

> MEG
> Go away. I'm praying.

> TOM
> I've been sent here.

She takes his hand.

                    MEG
Really?

                    TOM
Sent here to find you.

                    MEG
By who?

                    TOM
Heaven.

                    MEG
Are you making fun of me?

                    TOM
No. I need your help.

                    MEG
Why? What has happened to you?

                    TOM
God has spoken to me.

                    MEG
              (disappointed)
Ah, yes. Of course, I should have known.

                    TOM
He has given me knowledge of the Bible. But
I don't know what to do with it.

                    MEG
Poor man, my love, why has this knowledge
been given to you?

                    TOM
I don't know. I'm being punished, I think.

                    MEG
Yes, I see. Like me, you are doomed.

They move into a kiss, but are interrupted.

                    GUS
     So, you say you have some special information
     about the Bible.

Meg and Tom separate.

                    TOM
     Yes.

                    GUS
     And what is it?

                    TOM
     It's written in code.

                    GUS
     Fuck! Another conspiracy theorist! I'm going
     back to bed.

                    LEA
     And where is the key to this code?

                    TOM
     In the Book of Revelation. Chapters five
     through eleven: The Seven Seals. They are the
     code to unlocking the meaning of the Bible.

                    BOB
     And you've been—what—shown this code?

                    TOM
     Yes.

                    JED
     That's it? That's your big insight?

                    TOM
     Yes, it is. If the meaning of the Seven Seals is
     a mystery to you, you are not a servant of God.

BOB

Now, just wait a minute! I am a servant of
God! I was a God-fearing Christian before you
were even born, you suspicious little punk!

TOM

I'm sorry, friend, but the fact is you were not,
and you still are not, not if you lack an
understanding of the Seven Seals.

LEA

Wow. This is hardcore.

Anxious for her new lover, Meg tries to intercede:

MEG

Perhaps one could want to serve God without
really being able to serve God.

TOM

One becomes able to by learning the meaning
of the Seven Seals.

GUS

And, so, are you going to teach them to us?

TOM

Sure.

BOB

So, you are a prophet?

TOM

If you say so.

GUS

Hey! Don't give us the runaround!

TOM

I'm a sinner like many others. And I don't
know why this revelation was given to me.

MEG

The ways of God are not known to man.

GUS

Which of course could mean perhaps that
well maybe he is a prophet.

BOB

I confess I want to believe and, well, doubt.

EVE
(to Tom)

Will we have to wait long for the end of the
world?

TOM

Don't think like that. It's not a matter of
waiting. It's a matter of making it happen.

LEA

You are the lamb: "He that has prevailed to
open the Book."

MEG

The new Christ.

EVE

Is it you?

TOM

What do you think?

EVE, LEA, MEG
(approaching him)

We want to believe.

TOM

Then pray. Pray that I am.

He and the women are about to collapse softly into a tender orgy,
when—

                              JED
          Pervert! Rapist!

The women scatter.

                              BOB
                     (to Jed)
          Easy, friend.

                              JED
          He has molested my mother!

Meg rolls her eyes and turns away.

                              TOM
          I did not molest your mother.

                              JED
          You cannot deny it!

                              TOM
          I did have sex with your mother.

Everyone looks to Meg.

                              MEG
          We have tried to fulfill prophecy.

                              JED
                     (distraught)
          Oh, man.

                              TOM
          Isaiah, chapter eight, verse three.

                              MEG
                     (recites)
          "And I went unto the prophetess and she
          conceived and bore a son."

Bob looks at Gus, taps him on the shoulder, and the two of them step aside.

BOB

This looks bad.

GUS

The woman is seventy-three years old.

JED

And, besides, she's my mother!

LEA

Hey! The Bible tells us Sarah bore Abraham a
son at the age of ninety.

BOB

That was different.

LEA

Why was that so different?

BOB

The times! It was a different kind of world
back then! There were giants in the earth in
those days! And, besides, Abraham was the
chosen of God!

LEA

And is not our prophet equally blessed?

GUS

Well, that remains to be seen.
(to Meg)
Have you conceived?

MEG

No.

GUS

Well, then, obviously, someone here is *not* a
prophet!

The men laugh childishly until—

EVE

But I have.
> *(as they shut up and frown)*
I will have his child.

MEG

Why, you little tramp!

Everyone jumps forward and catches Meg as she runs for the girl, who cowers back and explains.

EVE

I was given a dream by God and told to give
myself to this man and to bear his child.

JED

> *(to Tom)*
Is this true?

TOM

Yes. The girl threw herself at me.

Meg falls to the floor, clutching her heart, and dies on the spot. The others step away and look on as Jed approaches the body, looks sadly down at his mother, and then challenges Tom.

JED

Raise her from the dead.

TOM

> *(at a loss)*
Pardon me?

JED

If you're the Messiah, then raise my mother
from the dead. If you can't, then I will.

LEA

He's insane.

JED

No! I have done the research. I have read all
the appropriate books and corresponded with
most of the acknowledged authorities. You
see, scientific research, backed by immense
technological and political support, is our only
remaining form of salvation, our only chance
to save ourselves from the perverted whimsy
of metaphysics, the brute unconcern of the
Almighty! Molecular genetics! Recombinant
DNA! Hybrid molecules and biotypes never
before seen in nature! I'm talking about the
artificial manipulation of the evolutionary
process! A new eugenics! Through genetic
engineering I have developed a process for
animating biologically functioning molecular
organisms. Yes! Don't interrupt! We must
interfere with that invisible hand of natural
selection and transcend the natural decay of
living tissue! God *wants* us to! I have
re-sequenced my mother's DNA. Observe.
Mother! Mother, come, rise and walk again!
Mother!

Finally, Meg rolls up off the stage and joins the others. Like them,
she's out of character and anxious to push on with the play. But
Jed is in a world of his own. He throws the flat of his hand against
his chest and gazes up into the lights.

JED
(triumphant)
We have at last wrested the secret of life from
the deity! Science has prevailed! The millennium
has arrived!

MEG
(confused, to Lea)
What?

LEA
He thinks you're his mother.

                             BOB
Can we just get on with this?

                             JED
Are you not my mother?

                             MEG
Give me that.

She takes the mic he is holding and walks away.

                             LEA
Pull yourself together.

They set up for a new scene and Jed is left alone, increasingly
troubled. He looks to Tom, who is the only one still paying attention to him.

                             JED
Is it true? Can this be true? Is this just a play?
Am I not God?

                             TOM
It is possible.

                             BOB
                     (anxious, to Tom)
I mean, you're absolutely certain he is not
God, right?

                             GUS
The poor man is retarded! Come on, let's go!

But Tom hangs back.

                             TOM
                       (calls out)
We are all retarded.

This is new. The congregation lingers, willing to hear more. Tom
moves amongst them.

TOM
(continues)
Each and every one of us is retarded. The first
step in receiving the Word of God is to accept
the fact that we are all retarded. We are all
mentally handicapped so long as we do not
comprehend the Word of God.
(to Jed)
I have seen God. Why? I'm not certain. But I
have seen God face to face and you, my
friend, are not him.
(to them all)
But you are one of us. And God doesn't care
if you're an idiot or a genius. He doesn't even
seem to care if you're a sinner. Look at me.
Why has God chosen me? Why has he picked
me out from amongst the crowd to do his
work? He must need a sinner, is what I think.
He needs someone to gather the faithful who
can't claim to be perfect. For, as it is
written in the Psalms—

LEA
(reads)
"Evils have encompassed me without number;
my inequities have overtaken me."

TOM
And I need children. Lots of children. Children
born here, far from Babylon, and raised in the
light of the Bible; a generation pure in mind,
body, and spirit, uncontaminated by the slow
decay of the outside world.

MEG
"Be not envious of evil men, neither desire to
be with them. For their hearts studieth
destruction, and their lips talk of mischief."

TOM
Bring me your daughters, the virgins

particularly. I will lie with them and make
them my wives.

                    BOB
Now, just hold on a minute. There are laws
around here.

                    LEA
Laws that are broken every day of the week.

                    EVE
And I want to! I want to have a baby for God!

                    GUS
Have you done your homework?

Eve turns away and sulks. Lea addresses the men.

                    LEA
There's nothing to be ashamed of. We're all,
you know, churchgoing people and everything.
I mean, after all, what's the big deal?

                    JED
               (flustered)
Well, the big deal is… You know!

                    LEA
You're just jealous. And you have dirty minds
too! Here we are, wanting to do something
selfless and beautiful; to create a generation
of righteous young souls, and all you can
think about is sex, sex, sex!

                    MEG
               (concurs)
Yeah.

                    EVE
               (timidly)
Yeah.

                              LEA
You ought to be ashamed of yourselves!
                    (to Meg and Eve)
You coming?

And the women float away upstage with Tom. Jed and Gus linger
aimlessly downstage as Bob pages carefully through the Bible.

                              JED
Nice floor, huh?

                              GUS
What?

                              JED
The floor: well made, nice color.

                              GUS
Low-grade particle board. And it's black.

                              JED
Look, I'm just trying to make conversation.

                              BOB
                    (reads)
"He shall have ten score concubines and
virgins without number…"

                              GUS
Now, these windows, that's another thing
altogether.

                              JED
Prefab.

                              GUS
No way!

                              JED
Yeah. Modular. A catalog purchase,
obviously.

                              BOB
"He shall scatter his seed and the earth
replenish…"

                              GUS
                         (to Bob)
Hey, what do you think, are these windows
prefabricated or custom made?

                              BOB
How are we going to feed all these divine
children?

                              JED
We can go into business.

                              GUS
What kind of business?

                              JED
We can sell used cars, for instance.

                              BOB
Have we come all this way, struggled all this
time to live in righteousness, away from the
temptations of Babylon, only to become, in
the end, used-car salesmen?

                              GUS
Import-Export.

                              BOB
Of what?

                              GUS
Cheap watches and calculators. I know a guy
in the Philippines.

                              BOB
Have we come all this way, struggled all this
time to live in righteousness, away from the

petty avarice of the outside world, only to become, in these, the final days, peddlers of cheap watches?

                    GUS
Yeah, I know. And, besides, there's not much money in it.

                    JED
Guns. We can sell guns.

                    GUS
Is that legal?

                    JED
Sure, as long as we pay for the license. We can buy the parts and build them ourselves. Lots of people do it.

                    BOB
Have we come all this way, struggled all this time…
          (pauses, concedes)
We do have to protect ourselves.

                    GUS
The outside world distrusts our motives.

                    JED
People have begun talking about the prophet having sexual relations with underage girls.

                    GUS
Not to mention their moms.

                    BOB
Let them talk! People can't believe in what they don't understand.
          (then, calculating)
We'd have to sell a lot of guns to feed all these kids, though.

GUS

But the children themselves are here to
help us.

BOB

To build guns?

GUS

Young people need practical skills.

JED

An idle mind is the devil's workshop.

Lea re-enters, upset and anxious. She looks to Gus, who hands her
a letter he removes from inside his jacket. She reads it and hands
it to Meg, distraught.

MEG
(reads)
Her ex-husband has filed a lawsuit.

LEA

He's an alcoholic and an unbeliever!

GUS

Be that as it may, he wants your daughter
taken out from under your custody.

LEA

I'll never let that happen!

BOB

He is afraid for the child's well-being here in
the presence of us, the faithful, in these, the
final days.

TOM

Send the girl away.

LEA

No!

                           TOM
                    (kindly but stern)
She will be returned to you in the end, when
all wrongs are made right.

                           LEA
She's all I have in this world!

                           TOM
And what are we then?

                           LEA
Forgive me.

                           TOM
I will give you another child. And you will be
a mother to the sons and daughters of the
millennium.

                           GUS
Wait a minute! She's my wife. If she wants
another child, she can have one with me.

                           LEA
Keep dreaming, asshole!

                           GUS
Shut the fuck up!

                           LEA
Get a job!

                           TOM
People! People! Easy! Settle down.

Lea buries herself in Tom's chest as Meg takes Gus aside.

                           MEG
It is certainly a hard thing to have God take
your wife away through death. But is that
really proof of loving God above everything

else? Is not this a more piercing test of your
faith? Isn't it more holy to have God take
your wife away now while she is still living
and have her enter into the arms of another?
Isn't it?

GUS

He is not God.

MEG

He never claimed to be God.

GUS

He claims to speak for God.

MEG

He claims God speaks to him. That's
different.

TOM
(to them all)
This much has been revealed to me: we are
all—women and men—married to God first;
it is wrong for you to have sex, even with
each other. Celibacy is a requirement of the
faithful, in these, the final days.

GUS

Yeah? And what about you?

TOM

I am forced to be a sinner. God wants it that
way. I am being sacrificed. I am taking on the
responsibility of sex so that the rest of you
can devote yourselves to better things.

Tom exits with Lea and Meg.

GUS
(to Bob)
What would you do?

BOB

If he is who he says he is, he is not doing
anything wrong; he's just telling the truth.
And if he is not who he says he is, then I
cannot bear to go on living.

GUS

I'm leaving.

Gus leaves the stage and sits up with the audience. Meg re-enters
and stands looking out at him.

MEG

He's jealous.

BOB

Divided.

Tom returns as well, watching Gus and the audience.

TOM

Why do you judge him so harshly?

MEG

He sows the seeds of doubt.

TOM

To doubt is not a sin.

LEA

He's a dangerous man.

TOM

That's what they say about me.
          (to Bob, of audience)
Who are these people? Why are they watching
us?

BOB

They've come to see if you are, in fact, what
you seem to be.

TOM

What is it I seem to be?

JED
(diplomatic)

They know about your many wives.

EVE

Our religious practices *are* hard for most
people to understand.

LEA

Of course, they're hard to understand! This is
not an amusement park! It's a place for the
faithful to be tested! Are our religious practices
something you, personally, find hard to
understand?

EVE

I'm only human. And they are confusing.

TOM

It's true, they are confusing and we are only
human. But remember, our aim is to do God's
work on his terms, not ours.

BOB
(also diplomatically)

They know about our guns.

JED

The guns were a good idea!

BOB

They keep asking about the guns.

TOM

What do you tell them?

BOB

The truth.

TOM

And what do they say?

BOB

They think we're manufacturing fully automatic weapons and they want to make sure we're paying the appropriate taxes.

TOM

Are we manufacturing fully automatic weapons?

BOB

No, we're manufacturing semiautomatic weapons.

JED

There's a difference!

TOM

There is?

JED

Different license! Different taxes! Totally different thing.

BOB

But the newspapers claim we stockpile weapons and are planning some sort of revolution.

TOM

Against whom?

MEG

Babylon.

TOM
(unafraid)

Well, let them come in and we'll show them our guns.

BOB
I did, but they refused the invitation.

JED
They're looking for an excuse to attack us!

TOM
Calm down. We have nothing to hide.

BOB
Well, you have, in fact, broken the law.

TOM
That's true: I have broken the law. But it has
nothing to do with the guns. It has to do with
their morality up against our morality. Their
sexual ethics up against our sexual ethics. But
still, we have nothing to hide. What we
believe in cannot be explained as quickly or
as easily as the outside world would like.

BOB
Look, I want to believe.

TOM
Then have faith.

BOB
I can't without proof.

TOM
Of what?

BOB
How much longer must we wait? You
promised us! Where is the millennium?
Are we all going to die for nothing?

TOM
Who says we're going to die? And I didn't
promise you anything. I told you what I knew.

                              GUS
                          (off)
What you knew and dared speak.

They all turn to see Gus come back to the stage, tired and drunk.

                              TOM
Our friend has returned.

                              GUS
No. I have been sent
Back
Sent back to warn you
I have been sent back by Babylon to warn you
I'm afraid.
For you, I'm afraid.
I confess
I want
To believe, but…

People pay big money to hear about you
On TV
And in the newspapers too I was interviewed
In a magazine, even, they took my picture and all
That.

I'm sorry.

They need to make an example, it seems, of
      some one
Or other
Of the faithful in these
The final days.

It is true, I admit
I doubt
But still, you are right to avoid them
This world of our neighbors in need
Anxious as they are for stimulation without
      end
And endless proofs, therefore, of abilities not

needed.

It is worse than I ever imagined
A population greedy for the first arousing
    glimpse
Of an imagined common decency in the throes
    of moral decay
A global community sick
With desire
And the desire to destroy
Desire, though desiring still
Each gut-rumbling detail
Or meaningless clue
To the supposed existence of the perfectly
    unspeakable
Ritualized sexual deviancy
Of you, the faithful
In these, the final days.

TOM

Thank you. We've been warned. You can go
now.

GUS

Babylon does not want me, it said
Photographs are more valuable.

They did not want me as I was
Useful at first
But only just
Curious thereafter and now spent.

They disgusted me and I, myself.
Here, see, this is the money I earned
And lost
On drink
To dull the ache of continued ambivalence.

I confess I insist I want
To believe
I cannot be damned

For my doubt, I think
Is needed

                    JED
The man's a wreck!

                    LEA
Traitor!

                    TOM
I'll go out and talk to them.

                    MEG
No! Don't!

                    JED
They can't be trusted!

                    TOM
But they'll listen, right?

                    BOB
And not hear.

                    GUS
Do not underestimate the outside world, my
friend.

                    TOM
                (frustrated)
We have nothing to hide.

                    GUS
That is, perhaps, true. But it is also beside the
point.

They all pause where they are, then break and deliberately take up
new positions. The date 1993 is projected on the floor.

                    JED
Go.

The cast begins a well-rehearsed and careful set of movements re-enacting a violent and confused event while striving to list the exact details of what they remember:

                    TOM
      The door was open.

                    EVE
           (to herself, remembering)
      Heaven opened up and I saw the world
      beneath me.

                    JED
      I told you to bring a gun.

                    BOB
      And you refused.

                    TOM
      I refused to bring a gun.

                    EVE
      And the angels were singing.

                    BOB
      You were showing off!

                    TOM
      At the door, I could see them.

                    LEA
      You saw them and called for them to keep
      back.

                    TOM
      I saw them running towards me and I told
      them to stay back.

                    JED
      There are women and children inside, you
      said.

TOM
But they kept on coming.

MEG
There were so many of them.

JED
Where?

EVE
Outside.

JED
Outside where?

EVE
Outside the sanctuary.

JED
What sanctuary?

EVE
In the temple.

JED
But where is the temple!

TOM
I raised my hands above my head.

LEA
A shot was fired.

JED
It wasn't me.

TOM
Then another.

MEG
You were hit.

TOM

I fell back against the door.

EVE

And they told me to wait and to live in hope.

MEG

Then I fired too.

LEA

You fell in through the door.

TOM

The door was closed and the bullet hit me—
here.

MEG

The children were screaming.

JED

I fired and saw a soldier go down.

TOM

I fell to the floor and heard the children
screaming.

MEG

The windows exploded and I ran to your side.

LEA

Get the children down to the chapel.

TOM

Keep your heads down.

MEG

It'll be over in a moment.

JED

They were carrying the dead away on their
shoulders.

                    LEA
They were praying down in the chapel.

                    EVE
"For Jesus has come down to us, but he is
waiting."

                    BOB
Bleeding.

                    TOM
On the floor, yes, I am bleeding.

                    EVE
          (points to Tom's wound)
Here.

                    GUS
               (reading)
"Keep awake and pray that you may not come
into the time of trial; the spirit indeed is willing,
but the flesh is weak."

They complete their enactment, pause, and fall from their poses.
They scramble for new positions, close to the floor, under siege.

                    JED
We had to defend ourselves!

                    MEG
               (ecstatic)
This is the Apocalypse! The coming of the
millennium!

                    TOM
             (in disbelief)
Do they really think they can get away with
this?

                    GUS
Apparently.

                    TOM

Tell them! Go! Tell them there is a law
higher than theirs! Tell them! And I will
forgive them!

                    GUS

They want to know what it will take for
you to release the hostages.

                    TOM

What hostages?

                    GUS

Us.

                    BOB

Are we hostages?

                    GUS

They say so on the news.

                    JED

We live here!

                    LEA

We don't want to leave!

                    GUS

Yes, but that is because you have been
brainwashed.

                    MEG

By who?

                    TOM

By me.

                    EVE

Have you brainwashed us?

Tom doesn't know. He looks at them all, wondering.

TOM

Was I wrong to tell you what I thought you
wanted to hear?

MEG

No.

LEA

Why are they doing this to us?

GUS

We killed some government employees.

TOM

They were attacking our home!

JED

They shot our prophet!

MEG
(reads)
"And when they shall have finished their
testimony, the beast that ascendeth from out
of the bottomless pit shall make war against
them and shall overcome them and kill them."

LEA
(hopefully)
This is the Apocalypse, then, isn't it?

TOM

It doesn't have to end this way.

GUS

Come away from the windows.

JED

They're getting ready.

EVE

For what?

BOB

To burn us down.

TOM

You do not know that!

BOB

We've been cheated.

TOM

There are things I can do. I'll surrender.

MEG

No!

EVE

Please, don't!

TOM

I'll make a deal with them—a compromise.

LEA

Then you will be just like them!

TOM

They'll kill us all! They'll kill our children!

MEG

But this is the Apocalypse!

LEA

And we are all going to heaven.

The women all kneel in prayer. Tom looks to Gus for help. Gus approaches the women.

GUS
(to Meg)
Take your children and get out of here.
(no response, moves to Eve)
Go! Run!

(no response, runs to Lea)
Send your children outside. They're innocent
and in danger!

But they stay where they are, deep in prayer. Stunned by this determination, Gus strides over to Jed.

GUS

Talk to them!

JED

And say what?

GUS

Those people out there are capable of anything!
They are not impressed by God!

JED

Well, I refuse to live in a world like that.

Jed sets down his mic and moves away to pray with the women. Gus looks over at Bob who is staring at the floor, despondent. Finally, Gus looks to Tom, sadly resigned now to all that is about to happen.

GUS

Say something.

TOM
(afraid and amazed)
"See how I burn in my love; how hungrily I
long. So is the lover's soul consumed with
indescribable fire; shot through with the
flames of heavenly light. There is no end to
this fervor and happiness as I push on
towards the object of my love. Death
becomes sweet to me as well as sure. See
how I burn in my love."

The performers hold their poses a moment, then break and leave the stage without ceremony. Lights out.